LAIRD HUNT

Laird Hunt is the author of six novels, a collection of stories and two translations. *Kind One* was a finalist for the PEN/Faulkner Award for Fiction and won the Anisfield-Wolf Award for Fiction, and his last novel, *Neverhome* ('A brilliant and breathtaking blaze of a novel' Clare Clark, *Guardian*), won the Grand Prix de Littérature Américaine and The Bridge Prize and was shortlisted for the Prix Femina Étranger. He teaches in the creative writing PhD programme at the University of Denver, where he edits the *Denver Quarterly*. He and his wife, the poet Eleni Sikelianos, live in Boulder, Colorado, with their daughter, Eva Grace.

ALSO BY LAIRD HUNT

Neverhome
Kind One
Ray of the Star
The Exquisite
Indiana, Indiana
The Impossibly

LAIRD HUNT

The Evening Road

VINTAGE

1 3 5 7 9 10 8 6 4 2

Vintage
20 Vauxhall Bridge Road,
London SW1V 2SA

Vintage is part of the Penguin Random House group of companies
whose addresses can be found at global.penguinrandomhouse.com

Copyright © Laird Hunt 2017

First published in Vintage in 2018
First published in hardback by Chatto & Windus in 2017

penguin.co.uk/vintage

A CIP catalogue record for this book is available from the British Library

ISBN 9781784703646

Printed and bound by Clays Ltd, St Ives Plc

Penguin Random House is committed to a sustainable future
for our business, our readers and our planet. This book is made
from Forest Stewardship Council® certified paper.

For the thousands

THE EVENING ROAD

OTTIE LEE

I was working the crank on the new pencil sharpener, feeding it fresh Ticonderogas, trying to get the points just right. Sharp enough was the idea so you could stab without pushing too hard, dull enough so the tips wouldn't snap straight off, leave important evidence behind. The personage I would introduce those sharp pencils to was my boss, Bud Lancer. I'd shed my heels and stocking-foot up on him when he was leaned back in his chair, deep into some afternoon snores. He was awful big so I'd take two Ticonderogas in each hand. Give out one chuckle when I did the work, another when I wiped the pencils clean. Bud, who was the one who had come up with the game, would laugh loud when I told him about it. I'd sit on the corner of his desk and swing my foot and shine my eyes over at him the way he liked it and hold up my perfect murder pencils and make him roar. Meantime, though, all the new machine was doing was eating up good writing implements and making my arm tired and obliging me to swear.

I broke another pencil, spit into my wastebasket, said, "Shit goddamn," and that's when Bud burst out of his office with a cigar in his hand.

"You can't tell me you haven't heard."

"Heard what?"

"About the lynching over in Marvel."

"The what?"

"Some cornflowers shot a cornsilk and set a hundred houses on fire and ran a rampage over the countryside. They got them over in the jail but they won't be in that jail for long. There's some boys going to get them out with sledgehammers if the sheriff won't open the door."

"And do what with them?"

"Didn't I just say it? They're going to hang them up like chickens. Pluck them first too."

Bud laughed and told me to put the pencils away, he would give me a ride over, we could go in his car.

"But I was planning on killing you with them first," I said.

Bud grabbed his hat, then groped in his desk for his keys. He said it wasn't time for games, that there hadn't been a real public lynching in Indiana in he didn't know how long. We ought to get on over there if we wanted a spot. He said for all he knew they would be auctioning off the good places beneath the tree, that it would be better than any picture show. If we wanted to see it we ought to get a start. I told Bud that I didn't know. Game or not, I had those pencils to sharpen and two policy-adjustment letters to prepare, not to mention I had to get dinner for Dale and there was things we needed from the store.

"Dale, hell," said Bud, taking a quick suck on his cigar. "If he ain't over there already you can bet he's fixing to go."

"You think?" I said.

"There isn't any thinking to it. You know when it comes to fun with cornflowers, he's always the first one in the line."

I gave out a laugh, but I didn't deny it. After all, Bud was Bud. He had been my boss for five years and six weeks, and one of the things you didn't do when you were in the workplace and he had a cigar in his hand, no matter how high his spirits, was contradict him. He had a cigar in his hand. I knew that when he got into his car and had started up the engine he would take one last long pull, then toss it out the window. Then he would put the car into gear and put his hand on my leg. One time, when he had his cigar in his hand and was fixing to get to some groping, I told him the file he had been talking about earlier was on his desk, which it was, but he had just the minute before said it wasn't. I argued the point and wasn't asked to go for any car ride with him that day or any other for a month. It got so stale in the office before the ship got steered back right, I thought he would fire me out onto the street. Then I'd have had to explain things to Dale.

Not that Dale, I thought, would have made anything out of it. Bud Lancer was the size of man to spit all the Dales of the world out of his mouth like old teeth. Once, of a Friday, I saw Bud pick a full-grown man up by his arms, turn him over, shake him good, then drop him like some pig trimmings into the trash. Bud Lancer had been a fullback to ruin them all in his high school days and now he was my boss.

"Come on, Ottie," he said.

"It's cornflowers they're fixing to put ropes on?"

"How many times do you want me to say it. Who else? Put those goddamn pencils away and get your things."

I thought the great big bright idea was to head straight off to Marvel, but Bud got stopped by some of the boys who worked in the print shop down the hall and they had to colloquize awhile about how it was going to be the biggest thing anybody ever saw. One of the boys, Charley Goodwin, who Bud Lancer had gone to school with and who hated Bud and who Bud hated right back, claimed to have been to a lynching when he was making a delivery down to Kentucky, but they all said they didn't believe him. He said whether they all believed him or they didn't wasn't any concern of his because it was true. They had hung a cornflower janitor right from a saloon sign, hadn't cut him down for a week. Folks down in this Kentucky town Charley said he couldn't remember the name of had set card tables out in the street and there had been a turkey banquet right there under the show. After the turkey was served a little girl sang "Dixie" and juggled five blue balls, then when the juggling was done they squirted the dead man with fuel oil and set him alight.

"Dinner right there under a dead man and a fire show on top of it," Bud Lancer said. "Did you hear that, Ottie?"

Then of course the boys had to chuckle on awhile about

that dinner and even if I didn't think it was that funny I chuckled along with them. Bud liked my way of chuckling. He always said that and the way I could fill out a shirt that wasn't even snug was what had got me my job.

Charley Goodwin would have liked to offer me a job if he had had any to hand out. He was just the press operator, though, and didn't have anything to offer but some bean-field charm and the orange ink under his nails. That didn't keep his eyes from tiptoeing over my way about every two seconds, and it didn't stop Charley, when we were finally fixing to leave, from asking Bud to let him ride with us to see the show.

"When hell freezes over and heaven takes in all the frozen chickens, Charley boy," he said.

"It might freeze over sooner than you like," said Charley.

"What's that supposed to mean?" said Bud.

"Means there's plenty wondering. Plenty asking questions."

"Questions about what?" said Bud and took a big step closer to Charley when he asked this. Charley shrugged and gave a nervous laugh.

"I'm just talking."

"Well, stop talking."

"You know I'm kidding you."

"Yes," Bud said, puffing his chest out a slice, "I guess I do."

Bud had me wait out on the street under Frisch's awning while he went to get his car. While I was waiting, I got to thinking about that little girl and that burning man and gave out a shudder started at the tips of my toes and went crab-walking up my legs because you couldn't help but wonder if they were going to burn and lynch them both over in Marvel, but then there came Sally Gunner out of the drugstore across the street. Sally Gunner was part cornroot through her father. She worked three days a week over at the lumberyard and said every other time you talked to her that she saw angels in the morning when she ate her breakfast. One of the angels liked to dip its finger in her oats and say if they were too hot or if they were too cold. Another lived in a painting Sally had of Abraham Lincoln. Sally said that angel was her favorite and that it would sometimes smile at her and tell her stories about heaven. She had little bitty eyes and a handsome hawk nose so it always looked like she had to be somewhere fast. I had known her about my whole life. She had been my first friend outside the Spitzers' Happy Home, which was where my own piece-of-shit old man would leave me for months at a time when he went on the road during my early years. Sally and me weren't friends anymore like the way we had been, but not one week past when I was coming out of that same drugstore she had caught me up in a hug right out on the street and said, "My Abraham Lincoln angel told me this morning there was something special on its way for you, something you can't miss, something that will make it all come clear!"

"Make what come clear?" I had asked her.

But she had just beamed and shrugged and gone hurrying along. That was Sally.

"Hi, Ottie Lee Henshaw!" she called out now.

11

"Hi, Sally Louise Gunner!" I called back.

I watched her hurry off on her way for a minute, her head full of who knew what, until a group of three other gals I knew came by all dressed like they were off to see the sailors and sit on their laps. One of them, Candy Perkins, had out her lipstick and mirror.

"Careful there, Candy, or you might trip and smack your head and wouldn't that hurt the sidewalk something awful?" I said as she passed.

"You waiting on big Bud Lancer to take you for one of his special rides, Mrs. Dale Henshaw?" she said right back.

It was about the hottest day there had ever been and I won't say that once Bud Lancer got me in his car and the air—oven-warm as it was—came streaming in I was sad to be sitting there. He had tossed his cigar out the window and had his left hand on the steering wheel and his right hand on my leg, and the air came flapping its buzzard wings into the window. He was talking about the lynching and getting there early enough for a spot and how his cousin had told him on the phone how they had hung a bloody shirt from the jail and everyone was riled up and so forth and so on, but I could tell by the syrupy tone of his voice that his hand wasn't going to stay happy just to set there aflop on my thigh. Sure enough, even though Bud kept saying he had to get me over to Marvel early enough for me to see it all, he turned off sharp when we came to the lane where he liked to take me.

The lane went past a pair of barley fields and a spread of run-down horse pens I expect they have long since knocked over or burned down. There was a stand of hickory trees next to a small pond where the frogs croaked like something big was about to jump in the water and set to destroying them. The pond wasn't big enough to fish so there wasn't ever anyone around. Bud was excited, what with the lynching to get to and all, so he went straight from putting his hand on my leg to making his try on me—which never went anywhere besides a fair amount of arm action and heavy breathing and pawing of my hair, especially pawing of my hair, since in those days it was long and thick and red—extra-quick. Still did all his regular damage to my makeup and the press of my clothes, though. Sometimes a blue jay came and watched us while Bud was at his pawing, but I didn't spot him that day. I missed him a little because he gave me something handsome to look at while Bud was at it. King of the countryside. Elegant and true. I thought I heard him give out a squawk a way off in the distance.

"Did you hear that jay?" I asked Bud when he was done splashing his sweat on me and had sat back in his seat.

"My name ain't Jay," Bud said.

That asinine remark was cause for some additional laughter and four or five pinches on my thigh. Then Bud's spare hand left my leg and went up to the steering wheel and he started to whistle like he'd just scaled the mighty mountain and planted his flag instead of scrabbling around in the rocks down on the flats. I have never liked a man to whistle and long ago trained up Dale to keep his whistling to himself, but even if Bud couldn't get it done, he paid me bonuses to let him act like he could, so I endured his whistle and looked out the window and wondered, now that I was off the clock and could think my own thoughts, what it was we had coming

14

when we got to Marvel. Once, as a girl, when I was still doing those stints at the Spitzers', I had seen a cornflower or some such who'd been selling bad tonic get beaten around the block, but never a lynching. A lynching was something else entirely.

I thought about what Sally had said. Maybe this was it, that special thing. Thinking about what it might be and what it might look like and what I might learn made me gander at my hands, then at my legs in their not-so-nice stockings, then at my feet in their good goat-leather heels, then at the soft backs of my hands, then at my nails, then finally at my long red locks. My hair weighed about twenty pounds if it weighed an ounce and through good times and bad, Dale had never allowed me to cut more than an inch of it at a time. And I expect if I had come in to work with it all cut off Bud would have just fallen right over backward and died. I straightened myself up then smiled big at Bud, but he wasn't looking. He was whistling and bobbling his head back and forth to the tune. Terrible sight and sound that might have got me glum but then it popped into my head that Candy Perkins and her friends had been heading to the show and that I might see them. And whether or not I had any special message coming, by God, I'd have a thing or two set to say to them when we got there.

I was fixing to try a line out on Bud to see what he thought when he belched and said, "We ought to go on over to your place and see if Dale needs a ride."

"If Dale needs a ride?"

"You said yourself his truck was broke."

I had said that and anyway this wasn't the first time after Bud had had his fun with me that he had thought of Dale. He liked to see Dale after he and I had been for a ride. He liked to clap him on the shoulder and throw him over a few play punches. Dale seemed to like it too. Bud wasn't just my boss, he was a big piece of cheese in the community and—problems with his people maker or not—probably could have sold Dale and any number of smiling others, I thought, tickets to get punched by him in the mouth.

"Let's go get that sorry critter, then," I said.

Bud gave a grin and turned off the blacktop and plumed the dust down the three or four roads to our house. I had thought Dale would be out in the shed or looking to the animals but there he sat on the one of our front steps that wasn't broken in a pair of clean overalls, just like he had been expecting us.

"I was waiting," he said when Bud pulled up.

"Waiting on what?" Bud said.

"On a ride to Marvel."

"Well, here you got you one."

"I can see that."

Dale didn't smile, because his teeth were so bad, but he raised his eyebrow and nodded then climbed in the backseat and we drove off again.

How did you hear about it?" said Bud. "Was it on the radio? My cousin said he heard a special announcement down at the barbershop. Said they put it through three times. You get the radio way out here?"

"Jesus Christ, 'course we get the radio out here. Don't we, Dale?" I said.

Dale didn't answer me. He had an awful lot of chaw in his mouth.

"I got to check on my pig," he said.

"You what?" said Bud.

"No, you don't," I said.

I'd known pigs all my life but that pig of Dale's scared me. She was giant-big and shiny and terrible smart-looking, glowed even in the noon light, would gander out the side of her head at you like she was a whale or a dolphin fetched up far away from its water and had a throat full of things to say you didn't want to hear.

I said no thank you again to seeing the pig, but Bud turned down the damn lane and we rode a bumpy half mile to the back forty where Dale kept that creature in a pig house he'd spent a year building out of wood we couldn't afford. You would have thought she'd cast a spell on him the way he swooned over her, that sow the size of three he kept swaddled up in perfumed straw and fed better than us. She was kind of just a huge puddle of pink half buried under her covers when we were still rolling, but when we stopped she hopped right up, trotted over to the rails, and gave a good deep snort you could hear straight over the engine.

"There she goes with that talking," I said.

"Be a jiff," Dale said.

"I got to see this," Bud said.

I didn't have to see it, I'd seen it plenty, but I got out and followed them around the car. Bud took the chance of being outside to hit Dale a couple of his good ones on the arm and Dale took a pretty good crack back at him.

"Here she is," he said.

"Good Lord in heaven," said Bud.

"I know it," said Dale.

"That's some piece of pork!"

"I'd like to see someone show me finer in this county."

"Landrace?"

"American Yorkshire. She come out all alone like she'd ate up all the others and not too far off this size."

"You could win a prize with a pig like that."

"Money in the bank."

"A bank full to bursting, she keeps on growing."

"She'll keep on."

While they talked sloppy like that, I looked at the pig and she looked at me. *You want to tell me something, don't you?* I thought. *You want to tell me things about this world or your world. About the world far away. You got things to say about me, I can see it. Nasty things. Whisper them at me, then chew off my ear. Bite off half my head. Lie down on me and sleep your beastly sleep.* I shivered, then laughed out loud and the boys looked at me, then went back to their talking.

There was a spot down by the creek kind of had indentations where I could fit my feet. I liked to visit there whenever it was my turn to look in on the monster. I had a view from where I squatted down, and once I got myself settled I looked out over the countryside. Corn and wheat and barley and more corn. It all looked burned up about right and had those wavy squiggle marks in its airs from the heat. I could see six barns and four silos from where I sat. It was good country. Not big but rich and you could live on it. Pull a life up out of its dirt. At the Spitzers', when we didn't behave, old Mrs. Spitzer would make us go out to the woods to do our business. There wasn't a one of us knew how to act just right so we were all out in the woods all the time. Wandering and bleating like sheep in a field. Pigs in the muck. Somewhere over there in about the direction I was looking was Marvel. You couldn't spit and hit it but you knew it was close and that thought made my stomach get the tinglies and the last time I had had them was when Sally had give me that hug and told

19

me I had something special coming. That something I now had my mind settled on that would make it all come clear.

When I finished up I hurried back over to the pig palace expecting they'd be in the car and raring to get to the show, but there they stood at the rails. Dale was pulling carrots from my garden out of his pockets and handing them to Bud, and Bud was handing them in to Her Royal Highness—carefully, like he thought he might be bit. One time I had put my hand on the flank that bulged out through the fence slats when you slopped her. I had thought she would be soft and hot, hotter than a star in its furnace, but she was hard and cool, cold almost, like the grave had already come calling and shoved some coffin in her.

"Get that pile of pork chops snacked up and let's get on the road," I said.

But Dale kept pulling my carrots out of his pockets and Bud kept taking them and that beautiful giant pig kept getting fed and that went on and on and on.

Now that he'd pawed at me then made it up all nice with Dale, who didn't even know he was being made up with, anyone had half a head could have guessed what Bud would come up with next, which was that he was hungry and wouldn't mind tracking down some food.

"Catfish supper today over to Ryansville," said Dale.

"Well," said Bud, rubbing those heavy hands over the steering wheel, "let's get over there and get us some."

There were so many vehicles at the Ryansville church it looked like they were having the lynching there. Cars and trucks were parked as far as a quarter mile up the road, and I said I didn't want my supper that bad but Bud went right ahead and stopped the car.

"You'll want your energy up for what we got coming this evening," he said.

"I'll want some energy left so I can enjoy myself is what I'll want," I said.

"Get out of the car, Ottie Lee," Dale said.

I didn't move a muscle until he added a "please" and would have probably kept sitting there until they either left me alone or hauled me out if about that time a whiff of fried catfish hadn't swished its way in through my window and set my stomach curious. I'd had exactly two crackers and a caramel candy since breakfast, and that catfish smelled so good I yanked the door open and shouldered Bud and Dale straight out of my way.

I was ready to do the same to anyone else ahead of me but when I got to the church I could see I wouldn't have to. Everyone was packed out onto the lawn and those clunkerheads weren't eating catfish at all. Some oversize boy in a brown suit didn't flatter his figure was standing on a soda crate and treating the smoky airs to a speech about democracy and freedom and corn crops and fresh flowers, or at least that was what I caught as I crossed the lawn and stepped into the church.

You would have thought there would at least be a few of them down in there to get their supper but I didn't see a soul as I followed the CHRISTIANS GIT YOUR WORLD'S BEST CATFISH HERE! sign down to the basement. It took my eyes a minute to adjust to the little lightbulbs they had hanging from the ceiling but it didn't take me long to see the piles of fish they had down there. They had so much catfish you had to stand a minute and take it in. And it wasn't just catfish — they had slaw and rolls and potato salad and two tables covered up in pies. There was steam in the air and everything came up glittery. It looked like you'd stepped into one of those old stories they were always telling us at the Spitzers' where Jesus gets Himself stirred up and casts a spell. Mr. Spitzer liked to lift his arms out to the side when he would tell that part. Lift his arms out and let his hair fall down over his face. In the church, they had a jar for your money and I opened my purse and took out some coins. Then I got my eye on the plates and stepped my way straight over. That's when I saw there were serving ladies down there. Three of them. Each about as old as Methuselah's uncle. They had on matching blue calico dresses and had covered their splash zones with aprons.

"Supping it alone this evening?" one of them said.

"I'm with two others," I said.

"Probably stopped to hear the speech," said another.

"I'm surprised you didn't stop yourself," said the third.

"I'm hungry," I said. "Hungry, hungry, hungry."

"I think every one of them up there is *hungry*," said the first.

"Is there some reason you aren't serving me? Money's paid and I'm standing here holding a empty plate," I said.

"Why, is there some reason we shouldn't?" said the second.

I studied on it a minute. 'Course there were reasons. I could think of a hundred but who in hell couldn't.

"I'm a sinner. How about you gals?"

"Oh, we've been friends with sin."

"But we found our way here."

"Yes, we did."

As the third one said this, the crowd outside let out a roar and about five seconds later it sounded like the host of the Apocalypse was starting down the steps.

"Do I get my catfish or don't I?" I said.

23

"Of course, dear," said the first.

"What would you like?" said the second.

"Make sure you pick out some pie and don't forget to praise the Lord before you eat it!" said the third.

I got my food, stepped back upstairs through the side door as the swarm went swarming in and made me think of the swine Christ cast those demons into and then thought of Dale's pig's cold flank and then sat down at one of the long tables they had set up on the back end of the lawn. It was a handsome place. Everywhere there was big trees giving out their shade and all around in the distances were the summertime fields. There wasn't any breeze but they had set out smoke buckets to work at the flies and mosquitoes. There were black-eyed Susans blooming all about and a great rose of Sharon bush standing at the back of the lot. My eyes lingered a minute on that bush. Because it looked a little, and just for a second, like the whole thing was covered in eyes instead of hardy pink blooms.

One of the things we'd had to do to earn out our days at the Spitzers', waiting on our shitheel wayward parents to return, was work the weekly ham-and-bean supper at the Baptist church. In the summer months I'd set tables as much as anything else and that had meant working out in a yard a lot like this one. Might have even had a rose of Sharon. Two or three times my last summer, as I was setting places, I got the feeling I was getting looked at but far as I could tell there was never anyone there. It was as strange a feeling then as it was now but I had an appetite and a plate of catfish in front of me so I looked away from the bush and down at my plate and liked what I saw. There is a curve to a piece of fried catfish that satisfies the eye. Leads you off to the rocks and reeds of the river where it once swam. I was about to set in to cutting at the center of that curve when a nickering voice nosed the air just behind me.

"Madam, may I count on your vote?"

Not only did the suit not flatter him but young as he was, he had on a false head of hair. He must have seen me looking at it because he reached up there quick and pushed it up straight.

"You bet you can," I said.

"I'm obliged," he said.

I'd said it because I wanted to get to eating and hoped he'd step off to some of the others coming out with plates but he just pulled up a chair next to me and sat himself down.

"Pretty lady like yourself," he said.

"Thank you," I said.

"You come to the occasion alone?" he said.

"Huh?"

"The supper, you're here just yourself?"

I pointed with my fork at the basement door and said I had a husband and a boss with me. He crossed one of his fat legs over the other and said that was a shame, that fate was cruelest to the kindest and so on. Then he said, "I expect you all are heading over to the lynching."

"That we are," I said.

"Have conveyance?" he said.

"We're riding in my boss's car."

"Lucky him."

I kind of squinted my eye, then looked down at my fish. It was sogging in its oils, its curve giving way.

"Yes, lucky, lucky him," he said and tapped at the table with his finger. It was a nice finger, long and fine as a lady's. I watched as his finger and its fellows tensed up and just about got themselves snapped off as he used them to shove himself upright.

"Best be off, I expect," he said. "I got buses coming to take them all over to the show and I'll have to organize them and may even captain one. They are coming at my expense, mind you. No one else will be out a nickel. I've been very lucky in my own humble way in this life. The great Governor in the Sky has been good to me."

I nodded. I could see there wasn't any more steam coming off my fish. That the juices of my slaw had run.

"It's a patriotic thing you're doing, madam," he said, and gave a little bow of his head that set his chin flaps to flopping.

"Waiting on eating this catfish?" I said.

"Going over to the lynching."

"Going to the lynching is patriotic?"

"Didn't you hear my speech?"

"I heard it. Some of it."

"And how did you find it? That portion that you heard?"

He gave a great big smile and more than I liked of a look at his pink gums. I have never liked someone showed too much gum. I shrugged. The smile fell off his face and into the brown grass.

"Was it that bad?"

"You want the truth, I missed most of it."

This seemed to perk him up. He leaned back, treated me to a small laugh.

"But you liked what you heard?"

"Yes, I did. It was real, real fine."

"'A torch of clarity to burn bright across the countryside during dark days'...That's got a winner's ring to it, wouldn't you agree? I worked hard on that part."

"You said that? About the lynching? The one that's happening today?"

"Yes, madam, I did. It is a difficult thing, a harsh thing, but it will burn things clear. Bring us back into balance. The hardest things always do."

"A bright light?"

"The brightest."

"Well, I'll give it to you," I said, "that part is pretty good."

He started to say something else, stopped, sneaked a look down the front of my dress, then showed me his gums again.

I'd finished all I had and slurped down a glass of iced tea to settle it before I saw a speck of Bud and Dale. I hadn't particularly thought they would come and sit down with me to eat—instead I had next to me a family of field-workers come for the cheap vittles—but I didn't think I'd find them standing, each one holding a plate in his hand, out by the road and watching a group of boys play break-into-the-jail either. It was some boys had got hold of chisels and mallets and had made themselves a hiding place out of a pile of old doors. One of the boys would sit inside and the rest of them would swing their chisels and mallets for all they were worth. When they had the thing down they would take the boy inside over to a tree and tie him up there with some rope and take turnabout at pretending to strangle him. Then they would untie him and start the whole thing up again.

"Let's get on over to the show before it starts needing a shave," I said.

"We're still crunching here," said Bud.

"As you can plainly see," said Dale.

They weren't the only ones out there watching the game with plates in their hands. There must have been more than a dozen thought it was right to eat their supper on the road while they stared at some juvenile display. Some of them standing there were Bud's relatives. Bud's father and his father's four sisters had set down more than two score souls on the earth. I'd met a goodly number of them because plenty of those fine individuals made it their weekly business to try and borrow from Bud. Matter of fact, as I stood there a tall knucklehead named Wendell Lancer leaned over Bud's way and I saw Bud reach for his wallet. I told Dale I was heading for the car and away from all the high excitement but didn't get any response outside the sun reflecting off the back of his greasy head.

The speechmaker had had on clean hair even if it wasn't his own, I thought as I walked to the car. And he'd had those nice hands to offset the suit. Not that the suit itself had been too bad. Just needed a man in it with a little less pie lard and gravy around the middle. Dale would have looked good in that suit, I thought. Dale, who wouldn't even wear a suit to his own funeral. Even if he had the right slim build for it, the right nice stretch of shoulder and those good slender arms. Dale, who wouldn't give a speech to save his own scratchy skin. There was something to a man with nice hands who could give a speech. "A torch of clarity." That was choice. And it was Sally's light. Sure as I was standing there. What else could it be? We all needed some clarity. Every little now and then. I ought to ride in one of that speechmaker's buses, get there quick, get there in style, I thought. I bet he'd let me sit in the front seat.

I was giving the proposition more than idle consideration

when I came up on an old man squatting on an overturned bushel basket in the middle of the road. He had a long white beard and wore a punched-in top hat. About every ten seconds he would stand up, shuffle around to the other side of the basket, and squat back down. He did this four or five times as I came up. I don't think he saw me until I was about on top of him.

"You coming or you going?" he said.

"I'm not coming so I guess that makes me going," I said.

"Going where, goddamn it?"

"Marvel, like everyone else."

"Then I can't let you pass."

"Can't let me what?"

"Pass," he said. He said it and reached down at the ground and tried to pick up some kind of a large-muzzle firearm.

"What if I said I was going so I could try to help those boys they plan to lynch?"

"Then I would stand up and accompany you."

"Well, that's not why I'm going. They're criminals. They deserve what they got coming."

"You believe that?"

"I just said it, didn't I?"

"Then you're as ignorant as all the others. Hand that up to me," he said.

"Why, so you can shoot it at me?"

He nodded.

"You live around here?" I asked.

He flicked a finger over to the right. All I could see was what

30

was left of a alfalfa field and a lightning-struck tree. I took another step. The old man put out one of his skinny arms.

"I can't let you pass. Can't let those buses they got coming in pass either."

"Why not?"

"I fought in the great Civil War," he said.

"You don't say it," I said.

"Indiana Nineteenth," he said. "I was at Bull Run and Gettysburg both. Those weren't the only ones. I was just a boy at the time but I carried that musket."

We both looked at the musket lying on the ground next to the basket.

"It ain't right to go to a lynching," he said.

"Even when they did it? Even when they are criminals?"

"How do you know they did it?"

"That's what I heard."

"You believe everything you hear? You got sheep hiding in that fancy red hair of yours? Saying 'bah,' making you follow along?"

"I don't like your tone."

"Bah."

"I don't follow anyone. I'm going 'cause I want to."

"You think that makes it better. Lord have mercy on us. Lynching ain't right."

"You said that."

"I'll say it again too, you red-haired piece of trash."

I bent over and picked up the musket. I wasn't any expert

on firearms but the barrel looked bent. Looked like the firing pin was out of commission too. I shook my head and handed it up and had to steady him and it both when he lost his balance and fell toward me off the basket.

"Take your hands off me, you filthy show-goer," he said.

By the time I walked on he had gone back to circling the basket, and the musket was again on the ground.

When Bud and Dale finally got to the car I asked them if they'd seen the old man.

"Crazy son-of-a-bitch," said Bud. "Said he wanted to fight me. Said he would kill me if I took another step toward Marvel."

"Bud picked him and his gun up and set them in some shade," said Dale.

"I think the sun had fried his head," said Bud. "He kept talking about Abraham Lincoln. And the Civil War."

"Did he say Abraham Lincoln?"

"And General Lee. He said even General Lee would have spoke out against a lynching! I about died laughing. Crazy as they come."

"That wasn't crazy, that was old. Crazy's different," I said.

"What do you know about crazy?" said Bud.

Dale gave me a look. It wasn't a mean look, might even have been soft, but I ignored it.

"Here come the buses," I said.

As Bud started up the engine, four bright white buses headed in the direction of the church rolled by.

With the lengthening of the day the bugs had come up and as we left Ryansville they started to populate the windshield with their splatter marks. When he was out for a summertime drive, Bud liked to bet on how many bugs his car would accumulate on a stretch of road. He started talking the game up now.

"Let's play how I could kill you instead," I proposed.

"Hell, that's something fun to do around the office, not out on the road."

"I'd kill you using pencils."

"You said that before we left. Let's bet on these bugs instead."

"Fresh Ticonderogas. A pair in each hand. Applied in opposing directions to your neck."

"You'd never make it up close enough to me."

"I'd do it while you was sleeping. You snore loud, Bud Lancer."

"I don't snore."

"The two of you play that at work?" said Dale.

"I already told you about that game."

"You told me about the guess-which-asshole's-calling game."

"I told you about both."

"I do not snore, Ottie Henshaw."

"Fine, you don't."

"Anyway, I'll bet it's going to be fourteen. Bugs, I mean," said Dale.

I snorted.

"That may be lowballing it, friend Dale," Bud said.

"That's my bet," Dale said.

"You sure about that?" Bud said.

"Oh, he's sure, he's always sure," I said.

"What's your bet then, Mrs. Know-It-All?" Dale said.

"Does that make you Mr. Know-It-All?" Bud said.

"You want to know what my bet is?" I said.

"We're all waiting, we can't hardly stand it."

I looked at the windshield. Evening was coming on and we still had a good thirty miles at least to Marvel.

"Sixty-seven," I said.

"Lord Almighty," Dale said.

"I'm going to say forty-two, kinda split the difference," Bud said. As he said this, a locust or some such hit the windshield with a *kerplang!* and left behind one of its wings.

For a while we counted each good smeary hit aloud and it wasn't long before we'd bug-smashed our way through Dale's sorry bet. Me and Bud laughed when we'd run past it but Dale crossed his arms over his chest and said just because we were past it didn't mean we'd get anywhere close to the numbers Bud and me had put up. I laughed but not too loud because

34

Dale had a point. That old crab apple chewed too much and paid too much attention to his pig but he did have a brain in his head. Bud was big and owned his insurance business and made deals on the side and had his car, but he was otherwise a cretin and Dale wasn't the village fool. He knew how to raise an animal no matter what its troubles and you didn't even want to ask him how many numbers he could multiply or divide in his head. My father had had a head for numbers and, when he wasn't too drunk, could read the pages of a book backwards about as fast as forward but Dale had him beat.

I expect it was because Bud was thinking along the same lines as these and hoping he could get out of a bet, even a friendly one he might lose, that when we saw Pops Nelson huffing up ahead at the top of the side ditch, he pulled the car over and hollered, "Need a ride to the rope party?"

"Don't think I've lost count," Dale said.

"Aw, let's leave off that, here's Pops," Bud said.

Pops, who had a great big sweat-soaked hat pulled down low on his head, hadn't noticed us yet.

"Get out and see if he wants a ride," Bud said.

"Get out yourself, I'm off the clock," I said.

"What's got you so grouchy?"

"Who says I'm grouchy?"

"The count is seventeen," Dale said.

"We're done with that," Bud said.

"Doesn't change the count," Dale said. "What did you say the winner got?"

Bud shot him a look and Dale said, "All right, all right," but I could tell in the way he said it that he figured he had notched up some great victory over me and Bud. Bud caught this too but he had other victories — or what he thought of as victories — in his pocket, and let it slide. He didn't let it slide so much, though, that he didn't slither his hand across the seats and poke my thigh hard enough to leave a mark. For his part of it, Dale, pleased with himself, leaned out the window and spit.

Bud got out of the car and caught up with Pops and a minute later brought him back. Pops had on his good overalls and a freshly starched shirt, but he had sweat so much it looked like he had just come up out of a dunking tub.

"Dale, Mrs. Henshaw," he said, nodding as he jimmied his way in. The car creaked a considerable amount as he set himself down.

"You in, Pops?" Bud said.

"I sure do appreciate it," Pops said.

Dale had shoved himself over to the side to give Pops more space. When the car had quit creaking and Bud had started it up again he fetched out his chaw pouch and offered it to Pops.

"Obliged," Pops yelled.

"Why are you yelling?" I said.

"He can't hear with the engine running," Dale said.

"What?" Pops yelled and scooped out a mouthful of chaw.

Dale knew Pops from the grain elevator and it wasn't long before the two of them were yelling back and forth at each other, both their voices nice and juicy from the tobacco.

Pops yelled, "Going to be a lynching," and Dale yelled back, "Yes, sir."

"I never have seen one yet," yelled Pops.

"No, sir, me neither," yelled Dale.

"You reckon they'll do them all at once?" yelled Pops.

"Why, was there more than one of them?" yelled Dale.

"Three's what I heard," yelled Pops. "Was it three, Bud?" he yelled.

Bud held up three fingers, then yelled, "Got a errand to run."

"What kind of a errand?" I said.

"What did she say?" Pops yelled.

"What kind of a errand?" Dale yelled.

"Hang on a minute, hang on a minute," Pops yelled. It took some doing but he got his hand in his front pocket and pulled out a fold-up ear horn and strapped it onto his head.

"Might as well save our throat cords for the party later," he said.

"We'll need them," Dale said.

"I was getting wore out on yelling," Bud said.

"Thank you, Jesus Christ, Lord of Heaven," I said.

We all took turnaround at considering Pops with his contraption on.

"That there looks like the end of a corncob pipe," said Dale.

"Or a hollowed-out statue of a mushroom," I said.

"My wife says it don't look quite Christian," Pops said. "She says it looks like some kind a devil horn."

"Anyways, I got a errand to run over to Hayley," said Bud.

"What kind of a errand?" I said.

"Is that what she was saying before?" Pops said.

We all laughed and Bud took us past the Russiaville turnoff, through woods and fields, then down the road and into town. I'd been through the residential part of Hayley once or twice and not thought too much of it and looking out the window at the scrappy lawns and houses didn't change my mind much. After a while, Bud pulled us up outside a circular building that looked kind of like an oversize hatbox set down next to a spindly creek could have been the hat's lost gray ribbon.

"You going dancing? Is that your errand?" said Dale.

"Dancing?" I said.

"Come on in and see," said Bud.

We went in under a canvas sign marked DANCE HALL and—after Bud winked at her—straight past the ticket taker sweating hard behind her counter. I couldn't have imagined anything worse to do than shuffle around up close next to someone in the heat they had for sale in there, but stab me straight down with God's sharpest stick if there wasn't a good dozen souls leaning into it while a orchestra of about four and a pony jingled out who knows what they thought it was on the stage. First the men leaned into the gals, then the gals leaned into the men. There was sweat splotches on the floor. Looked like you had to raise your arms up a lot.

What they needed was a real orchestra, some boys really knew how to blow and strum. Or a Victrola. Lord, even just that. Dale had got me one for our first anniversary. Bad off as we were, I had ten records I could plop down on that fine machine. You ever hear Hoagy Carmichael on the Victrola? It just doesn't get any sweeter. Never mind what new player machines they have now. I don't care about those. Dale liked that Victrola plenty for a while because after we'd listened to it and taken a turn or two his chances in the bedroom improved. He couldn't dance worth a tin nickel but my good Lord, when I had some arms around my waist how I could make my dress float across the room. If I danced or twirled long enough, worked up enough heat and had my head set to spin, I liked to see Dale Henshaw coming at me. Dale Henshaw had his charms. He was chawing out his teeth and didn't wash as frequent as he should but there was something to be said for a man who could move quick like he could and fly above you like a bird. He was tender in the bedroom. Just like sweet pasture butter with his ways.

When we were courting and well past that first year of our marriage he had sung songs and memorized poetry to say to me. Poetry! All it had taken was me telling him one night early on after we'd been at some whiskey that when my father, fresh from his final sales show in Iowa or somewhere and still wearing his suit, had come to take me away for good at last from the Spitzers, he had got down on a knee, spread his arms, and given up a sonnet. Didn't matter that it was a sonnet he'd made up to try to sell strawberry tooth powder, Dale heard this and the next day he came walking out of the field with a flower in his hand and a poem in his mouth. Prettiest thing you ever heard. Prettier than my father's sorry poem. Especially since when my father had bent his knee and said it he had been so drunk he hadn't even noticed I had whip burns on the backs of my legs. Those days of poems and Dale coming into the bedroom after me were done, though, and now if I put the Victrola on all it did was make the dogs bark. Doesn't matter how good you look or how nice you dance, you push a man away enough at just the wrong minute, he starts to turn his thoughts in other directions. "Come on, now, honey, let's make us a family," Dale had used to say, and he had said it kind, but for the better part of the past year I had made him stop. 'Course I had. There's things you can't chance. Now I looked at him. He was rubbing at a brown patch on his pant leg. Chaw stain. Probably thinking about his evil pig. I looked at him long enough that he looked back over at me.

"Staring contest," I said quiet.

"You know you can't win at that," he replied.

This wasn't true. Well, at least not all the time. We didn't dance much anymore, and he had given up trying to follow me into the bedroom even if we did, but we did still lock eyes at each other from time to time.

"Right here, right now, Dale Henshaw, let's see what you got," I said. But he was back to rubbing at his pant leg.

While we stood at the side, Bud walked up to a man with one of those ugly rat-whisker mustaches sitting on a blue chair at the far corner of the dance floor. He was holding a wore-out bullhorn and fanning at himself with a piece of drippy cardboard. It was either one fly or two that was worrying his head. The man didn't even look up when Bud leaned over and started to whisper in his ear, but after he'd heard what Bud had to say he shot straight up off his chair and yelled into the bullhorn: "Lynching over in Marvel!"

There wasn't a one of those cobs of corn didn't straight-away stop leaning back and forth into each other and start making plans about how to get to it quick. There was some pretty girls out on the floor and you could see how their nifty ways got to working in Bud's eyes. Dale had quit scraping at his chaw stain but if he was looking at anything it wasn't those ladies. A wandering eye wasn't one of his sins. The bull-horn man shook Bud's hand until it about fell off and then he shook Dale's, mine, and Pops's.

"Errand accomplished, folks," Bud said, all proud and

taking one more look at the dance hall, which was already starting to empty out. The band had kept playing a while after the announcement but now even they were packing it up.

"That was some errand," said Pops, whistling appreciatively as we went out through the crowd.

"Cousin of mine and business associate of the tin can runs this place was at the catfish supper, asked me to swing by, said it might boost future business if the dancers heard here about the happy event," said Bud.

"I expect they'll all head over," said Dale.

"Yes, I expect they will," said Bud, pleased as Punch with himself and all but licking his lips over some of the sweaty dresses scurrying by. "They will and when they're over there having the best time of their life tonight they'll think of this place and round up their friends and come back for more."

When we got out we had to stand and wait while all the parked cars unsnarled themselves. Bud talked on about opportunity, then set with the considerable saliva in his mouth to offering up commentary on the ladies he'd seen. One had had legs and the other had had arms and a third had had a face.

"Put a nickel in her mouth and I bet she'd talk to you with that face too," I said.

"I thought that one in the pink dress had a purty look to her," Pops said.

Bud took a peek at Dale, who was cleaning some crud off his shoe with a stick, then took a peek at me, first at my face and then at the rest. Then he shoved his hands into his pockets and let out a good long whistle.

"Lord, I love doing business," he said.

"Let's get on now," Pops said.

"I want my staring contest, Dale Henshaw," I said.

Then we all got back in Bud's car.

We'd gone only about six and a half yards down the road from the dance hall when the man had been holding the microphone came trotting after us with a bag. Bud stopped the car and leaned his head out the window and the man looked both ways down the street then pulled out three pretty pint bottles. He handed them over and Bud thanked him loudly and the man said, "From the boss, he says he'll see you over there! And I will too!" and trotted over to his own car. Bud was neck-holding the bottles and he pulled them back inside. "That errand idea just keeps looking better and better. Anyone besides me feeling thirsty?"

Bud gave a whoop, tossed two of the pint bottles into the backseat, took a swig of his own, and gunned the engine. Then he handed me his bottle and put the car in gear. I took a sip and spilled some of it on my chin when the car lurched. I had another sip and got more of it down. I can't drink as much as I once could but I don't disagree with the taste, even now. Bud was staring at my chest as I drank. He had that greedy look he couldn't do anything worth talking about with in his eye.

"That's the good stuff, Ottie," he said.

"Well, then, you better have it back," I said.

"Take another swig, take another swig," he said.

He gave a wink and let his hand climb up my leg. Dale and Pops had their bottles in the air and were sucking at them like calves at the teat.

You would have thought it ought to have been dark by then, but it wasn't evening by a long mile. The bugs kept coming to their end on the windshield but not even Dale was looking to that now that he had that pint bottle to play with. He hadn't been much of a drinker when we first met but he had sure turned that around. And of course I'd learned first thing from my father how to throw them down. Matter of fact, morning of my sixteenth birthday, he had come into my room, dropped a bottle onto the bed beside me, and said, "Let's drink to getting drunk." And Lord, we had. Instead of cake there was just a day of heaving in the bushes and spitting liquor on the charred remains of the birthday card my incarcerated mother had sent.

Dale and Pops were clinking bottles with Bud and drinking it down and singing driving songs. Bud and Dale couldn't carry either end of a tune, but Pops had a sweet voice. I have no doubt it fetched up fairer to me because I'd had my turn at Bud's bottle, but then that's the way the wood vine twineth with most things. I once heard a preacher had come to lay down some Christian law at us miscreants say eyes don't see and hearts don't feel until they get switched on. Bud's and Dale's ears hadn't had their switch for good taste turned on and they kept caterwauling, so I told them to shut their hamburger holes and listen to Pops. Bud gave me a look and Dale gave me a kind of half-assed pinch, but they did quit trying to sing.

Pops, with the floor to himself, took out his ear horn so it wouldn't throw him off and gave us "The Lonesome Valley" and "In the Pines," pretty as you please. It was while he was finishing up the second of these and drawing out the word *shiver* that Bud got started on mouthing things in my direction. I didn't catch what he was doing at first so I missed the gist and he had to mouth it again. To be sure about what he had said I had to mouth it back. This made him mouth his thing again at me, only it looked different this time. I mouthed the part of it I hadn't understood and he shook his head and slapped at the steering wheel.

Something, he mouthed.

What? I mouthed back.

Pops was on "Amazing Grace" now and working it hard with his eyes closed when we went up and over a rise and Dale said, "Jesus Christ!" I thought sure he was sore about all the mouthing going on but he was looking straight past us out the windshield at a pair of dogs trotting dainty-legged down the middle of the goddamn road. It was bloodhounds — big floppy-ear things — and I swear to heaven they each one of them had a necktie on. We were about thirty feet from running them down when Bud got his head swiveled around from looking at me and at Dale and hit the brakes and swerved and sent us sliding half sideways on some gravel patch, then back straight onto the blacktop. We kept skidding and there was a loud popping sound and Bud said, "There goes the tire," and Dale said, "Hold on now, Ottie Lee," and I held on and the whole car started juddering and there was a wet-branch sound of metal getting snapped and a smell of scorched rubber. I felt Dale's hand press hard on my shoulder like he aimed to shove me straight down through the car seat, and Pops kept singing loud like he was the radio, and up ahead and farther and farther away those dogs went trotting with their ears and neckties flopping back and forth like they hadn't seen or heard us either one.

You think I'm stupid, don't you?" said Dale. He said this to me after the dogs had disappeared and Pops had quit singing and opened his eyes and looked around and put his ear horn back in and said, "What in hell just happened?" We told him, then told him again because he said he couldn't believe it and Bud said, "It's a day of marvels is what it is," and no one laughed at his little joke so he set to cursing the dogs and whoever their owners were and the rest of the world while he was at it. We all took slugs of whiskey to settle ourselves and laughed at how it still felt like every part of us was shaking, then climbed out of the car.

"No, in point of fact, that's one thing I don't think about you," I said.

"You think I don't know what's going on?"

"Well, what is it you think is going on?"

"You must think I'm as dumb as a donkey doing its business in the rain."

"What's the rain got to do with it?"

"It's a figure of speech, Ottie Lee."

"Like in a poem. Why don't you say a poem to me?"

"*Recite,* Ottie Lee. *Recite* is what you do with a poem."

"Thank you, my beloved. Why don't you *recite* me a poem."

"The hell I will."

He had his hands in his pockets, and one of them had just been on my shoulder in the car, but I reckoned just about any second it or the other would come out and hit me. That's the way it got done in those days. Dale had hit me with a salad bowl just the past autumn. That was after I had told him at the supper table that he and his ideas about us having children were going to have to stop. Right there and right then. He asked me if I truly meant it, and I told him he knew when I said something with the bark on it I meant it, and he asked me if I had lost my marbles and I told him maybe that was exactly right, maybe that was just it, maybe I had. He said a child was what we had always wanted and what we had always aimed for and now we had a little money set aside and it was time to get to it and we had waited plenty long and so on and so forth. I said having children wasn't everything and maybe it wasn't much of anything. I said he ought to look at Bud, who'd lost wife and baby both to the Spanish flu and hadn't ever looked back. "You think that's true, that he never looked back?" said Dale. "She left him with that business, set him up good," I said. "The daughter did?" said Dale. "You know what I mean," I said. "Maybe I don't," he said. "Maybe you're an idiot," I said. "Hush on this now, Ottie Lee Henshaw," he said. "I don't want your last name when we're in the middle of a argument," I said. "Hush now." "Sure I'll hush. I'll hush

49

and get down on the floor and hunt for my lost marbles." I spit a little — or maybe it wasn't such a little — when I said this, right there at our kitchen table, and a glob of my spit got on his hand and he picked up the salad bowl and gave me a good crack on the side of the head that knocked me off my chair. That hadn't stopped me from getting up and giving it to him with a skillet and a china plate and a salad fork. I didn't back down.

There we stood on the roadside. Bud was under the front of the car and still cursing the dogs. Pops was humming. Dale looked at me and I looked at the ground and spotted a rock. I'd have picked it up and used it on him too if he hadn't said, his voice thick, "Let's have that staring contest now."

"You'll lose."

"Oh, you think you can beat me? It'd be a first and you know it."

"First, hell," I said, my own voice thick.

We had our heads about six inches apart; his two little eyes had turned into one normal-size one. He had taken his hands out of his pockets and rolled up his drooping shirtsleeves. I could smell the flecks of wintergreen chaw he had on his lips. His skinny eyebrows were all beaded up with sweat and I thought of how he had said, "Hold on now, Ottie Lee," when it had looked like we were in trouble, and I got this feeling come creeping over me something powerful that I wanted to kiss him. Kiss him maybe just on the cheek like I had used to. Before. Before I told him he needed to keep his pecker to himself or that he could share it with his pig if he wanted to. He had given me a crack across the face for that too. I had a mouth on me in those days. I'll never deny it. Just a little kiss. Right where his stubble stopped. Maybe then he would have given me one in return. Only that would have meant getting chaw flecks on my cheek. I bit a corner of my lip. Flared my nostrils. Focused back on the task at hand.

"Come on over here and take a gander at this sorry state of affairs, Dale," said Bud.

"Attending to business," said Dale, his eyes not blinking, not leaving mine.

"Is this what the two of you get up to? Should we turn away? We witnessing what you do during your private time?"

"Mind your business, Bud Lancer," I said. And I almost told Dale right then and there what it was he was already suspecting but had only half right. Told him so Bud could hear me telling it. And Pops as a witness. Who could tell Candy Perkins and all the other rumormongers that it was all just farce and shadow play. Only then there would have been a fight, because what else could there have been. Some of it was true. The driving and pawing part was true. And it wasn't the kind of fight Dale could win. I'd tell him later. I would figure out a way to tell him where it was we were getting our extra few dollars from each month and why he didn't need to let it worry him. Or not worry him too much. It was a mess. But not my biggest one. Not even close. Then I said, "Shit in a bucket!" because I'd let my eyes drift away from Dale's.

"I want a rematch," I said. "I demand it."

Dale smirked. He reached out his finger and gave my forehead a tap. Just a light one. He said, "We'll talk later, wife of mine." Then he put his hands back in his pockets, winked, and went around to the front of the car.

While Dale helped Bud, Pops kind of lolled against the side of the car with his pint. It was shady where he was so I went over and leaned up next to him. He offered me a taste and I didn't say no. What he had in his pint wasn't as good as what Bud had in his, which figured, but you couldn't complain about it not getting the job done.

"Fine evening," said Pops.

"Sure is," I said.

"Too bad about Bud's vehicle but it's nice we didn't hit those dogs. I like a good dog. I don't care what Bud says. Who do you think dressed them up in neckties?"

"You tell me and we'll both be wiser."

"Well, I sure wish I'd seen them. Running straight toward Marvel. Goddamn."

"Probably there by now."

"What color were the neckties?"

"Red and gold."

Pops smiled and sighed. "Colors of the sun. Lord, I bet that sun will be streaming 'cross the courthouse square. They'll cheer when those dogs get there."

We'd picked a pretty spot to be stuck. There were crows

fussing out over the corn waving its early August ways in front of us and there was a little rise looked like a pillow the evening sun was resting its head on. There were delicate bugs flying in the soft light and flowers looking less wilty now that the day was letting down. The sky had a color to it that you didn't see too often. There was some purple in it but also some pink. There was yellow but there was also orange and brown. Count the colors those bloodhounds had been wearing and it was like a springtime field full of flowers. There's no place in the world for a sunset like the Indiana countryside. I had always loved Indiana. Loved it for better and poorer. There wasn't anything changed about that. There still isn't.

"Too goddamn hot, though," said Pops.

"Hotter than a brick bastard," I said.

Dale and Bud were talking about the spare tire that wasn't in the trunk and about the repair kit Bud didn't have and the axle that was almost surely broken anyway.

"Long and short of it is we're fucked," said Bud, coming around the car to put his foot on the running board next to us.

"Comes a car," Dale said. Sure enough, there was a big black car made Bud's look small coming down the road. It slowed and who sat behind the wheel but Charley Goodwin with the orange ink under his nails.

"Well, now, looky here," he said.

"We got into a skid," Bud said. He didn't say anything about the dogs and none of the rest of us did either.

"Sorry state of a situation," said Charley.

There was about five more-or-less jackasses in the car with him and more than one of them had bottles of something too good-looking to have come out of a brown paper bag.

"Uncle's car on a loan," said Charley. "Bud's not the only one got family around here."

"She's a fine one," said Bud.

"You got any extra room in there?" said Pops.

"Full up, Pops," said Charley. "Though I expect if we squeezed, old Ottie could climb in."

"Squeezed what?" one of the men in the car said. This was cause for considerable laughter and bottle clinking in the vehicle. I couldn't tell if it was Dale or Bud who told them to shut their mouths first.

"Now, now," said Charley, "no one's looking for an altercation. Even if we got the numbers on you."

"You think you got the numbers, why don't you all come out of the car and let's count."

"Naw, Bud," said Charley. "We'll cede you the field. But it's probably you pretty soon going to need to be doing some counting. The green-paper kind. That's what I heard."

"Anybody's going to be doing any counting on our side ought to be me," said Dale.

"Shut up, Dale," said Bud.

"Shut up yourself," said Dale.

Bud ignored this and turned back to Charley. "You back on that?" he said.

"Just talking, like I said earlier," said Charley, giving out a laugh didn't sound so nervous now that his back wasn't against a wall. "You know how word flits around. It floats and it flits."

Charley laughed again and made his hand and fingers flap through the air.

"Anyways, let's get this crate rolling or we'll miss all the show," said one of the screw-tops in the backseat.

"Wouldn't want to miss the show, now," said Charley, pulling his hand back into the car. "We've already been having adventures along the road. Haven't we, boys? Dark's coming on. You sure you don't want to climb in here, Ottie? Got a spot next to me," he said.

"In your fanciest dreams," I said.

"Happy hoofing, then," he said and drove off.

Bud had turned thoughtful—no doubt meditating on whatever business troubles he was about to have—so when Pops and Dale set in to swearing at Charley's taillights disappearing down the road, he didn't join in.

"Fact is, we had better get to walking," he said.

"Back to walking, I'll be damned," said Pops.

"I'm not walking an inch," I said.

"Anyone wants to see the show had better dust off their boots," said Bud.

"I got on heels," I said.

"We'll catch a ride here before long."

"Catch a ride, my red ass," said Dale.

"What are you getting contrary about anyway?" said Bud.

Dale had clearly forgotten about the idea of us talking it over later and was looking long daggers from Bud to me and back to Bud.

"There's all kinds of ways to catch a ride, ain't there?" he said.

"What in hell are you talking about?" said Bud.

Dale gave him one last look, then spit.

"That's what I thought," said Bud.

"Come on now, boys, put the pistols back in your pockets, this ain't getting us any closer to the big show," said Pops.

"You done?" said Bud.

"What was Charley talking about?" said Dale.

" 'Bout things that weren't any of his business. Or yours. Things he's wrong as rain about. Now, are we going or aren't we?"

"Let's all take a drink," said Pops.

"I'll drink," said Dale.

It took some coaxing but Bud got a grin going on his face and the three of them fetched up their pints and drank. When they were done, Pops and Bud pointed their bottles in my direction, but I walked over to Dale and grabbed my drink out of his. This made Bud and Pops laugh and after a while Dale let his scowl drop and joined in. Joining in for him meant raising his eyebrow, clucking his head up and down, and spitting extra out through his front teeth. He wasn't dumb or stupid or even an idiot neither, and he'd stood up more than a little to Bud and Charley both. Plus he had put his hand on my shoulder, then beat me again at staring. Funny what you fall into in this world. Love and its ways. I leaned over, puckered up, and gave him that peck on his cheek.

Some way or other involving their pint bottles, they got me to agree to walk, so we posse'd up and set off down the dusky road. Now and again a car would roll by but never a one of them stopped. Pops said he thought it was probably because they didn't have any space like Charley hadn't had, but Bud, who was back to being mad at the dogs, and Dale, who was still grumpy despite my attentions, both said it was because they were bitches and bastards, plain and simple, every one. There was a good amount of glum talk about how long it was going to take us to walk to Marvel, where the bright torch was burning for others' eyes and who could have said how much fun they were all already having getting ready to climb up their ladders and dangle their ropes. Bud said Marvel had always been the town to have fun in — knew it for a fact since he had a sister living over on the outskirts — and Pops said he couldn't agree more. They knew how to laugh in Marvel and always had the freshest jokes. Bud asked Pops to tell one of the ones he had heard as long as it didn't involve dogs, but Pops said he couldn't call any to mind. Bud said he couldn't either. They asked me if I knew any but I was too hot to try and hustle something up.

"Still, that's the place to go for fun," said Pops. He said he had heard that the very day before there had been a human-fly display in Marvel and that five thousand people had turned up to see him climb a five-story wall.

"They have the space for it in that fine downtown. My sister says they're planning to expand, says maybe I ought to open another office there when they do, and never mind the rough times the papers say we're living in," said Bud.

"I reckon people can do their dying there without you," said Dale.

"Oh, they'll die easier with a fair policy in their pockets! Gives them peace of mind."

"Maybe you ought to slip a policy into the pocket of those boys they're planning to pull up to heaven."

"Wouldn't make me any money to do that. Tell you what, though — and fuck Charley Goodwin — after people get their good look at old Daddy Death tonight, I bet the phone will be ringing tomorrow, ringing right off its hook."

"Daddy Death?" said Pops.

"The big daddy," said Bud.

"Jesus Christ," Dale said.

Every fifty feet or so Pops would take off his hat, twist it up until the sweat dripped out, then pull it back down on his head. His ear contraption made it look like he was a half robot out of one of the magazine stories Dale sometimes read. This past early autumn he had been setting in the front room by the stove reading one and chuckling his ugly chuckle when we'd had a knock on our front door. Found a lady standing there with a heavy coat on even though it was warm out and there wasn't any chill. "May I come in, please?" the lady had said. I said it too now, out there in the blast heat, but nobody noticed. So I said it again, like I was in a trance. I had my hat off and was using it for a fan. Bud left off bragging on his business prospects, since not even Pops was pretending to listen, and started into some story I'd already heard too many times about how he had used to box on the undercard at the Cadle Tabernacle, but I interrupted him.

"I need a drink of water or I'm going to die," I said.

Bud said there was a store not more than half a mile up the road and we could get all the water we wanted and probably some fresh pints too.

But the place where that store was supposed to have been came and went, and they all one by one threw their empty pint bottles away into the high grass. We walked past sleepy pigs, sleepy cows, and sleepy horses. We walked past dying houses and dead barns. The mosquitoes came out thick every time we passed a stand of trees but Pops had some anti-mosquito salve and we all got greased up pretty good. With that situation more or less under control, there was a festivity to the evening that couldn't be denied. The birds were singing their last songs, the late clouds were bunching up nice and fat, squirrels chirped and chattered in the trees. As we inched closer to Marvel we got passed by more lynching-goers who hollered and cheered when they saw us, even if nary a one of them stopped when we hollered back. One truck had cans tied to its tail that clattered and bounced as it rolled along. Another was stuck all over with yellow roses so thick you couldn't see what color it was. I thought I saw Candy Perkins, or some other of her species, trollop on by in the passenger seat of a roadster, but I couldn't get a good look. Then along come a hay wagon filled to its scratchy brim with couples all snuggled up together under blankets. It looked like they'd took a wrong turn out of Halloween and ended up in August.

Snug and happy as they were, those hay-wagon couples called out for us to climb aboard and join them but the driver said he couldn't take any more load. Bud said it was true it looked like the tires were about to burst their sides. The subject of tires got Dale and Pops to complaining about walking again after the hay wagon rolled off, and after a while Bud spat and cracked his knuckles and told them to shut up.

"Tell you what, you think you can take us both?" said Dale.

"Yeah, what do you say? You think you could?" said Pops.

"Aw, I could take you both and her too, even if she had some of her pencils ready to poke at me with," said Bud, pointing at me.

"What kind of pencils?" said Pops.

"What in fuck does it matter?" said Dale.

"Ticonderogas," I said.

"I get the best," said Bud. "Buy them by the box and get a discount."

"Now he's bragging about his pencils," said Dale.

"They are pretty good pencils," I said.

This made Bud and Pops laugh, and Dale told them they could go fuck themselves with Bud's fine pencils if I could spare any, and I said if we had a goddamn car and not a wreck left by the side of the road I'd go straight over and get some, and Bud cracked his knuckles again, and Pops made a comment that set Dale to chuckling, and we all stopped to rest and squabble a speck under an oak tree.

"Either one of you two want to arm wrestle?" said Bud.

"I'd of laid you flat down when I was younger," said Pops. He was looking up at one of the long low oak branches when he said it.

"Listen," he said. "You're all laughing at me, old and fat as I am, but I'll tell you what. You want to see something, help me get up on that branch."

Dale said, "No one is laughing at you, Pops."

"Never mind if you ain't. Help me up. I'll show you something. I wasn't always a old fat thing. It's not just singing I know how to do."

"You ain't that old, Pops," I said.

"Let's save the trees for their lynching work," said Dale.

"Come on, let's help him up, he wants to show us something," Bud said. "I want to see it."

In the end it was all three of us helped push him up the tree and onto the branch. He sat there huffing a good long stretch, louder than all three of us put together, and I thought maybe that was it, that was his trick, to be fat and ear-horned up in a tree. Which you'll admit wouldn't have been just the small end of nothing.

Still, there was more to it, and when he got his breath back he said, "Now you all think I'm decrepit, watch this. Watch good. And remember when I'm doing it that I used to be able to do it and plenty more on a wire."

"Is that true?" I whispered to Dale.

"Don't you have some pencils to sharpen?" Dale said.

We watched. Pops groaned and huffed and got himself onto his feet.

"Easy there, Pops," said Dale.

Pops gave out a little laugh, then he lifted his arms straight out from his sides and spit some chaw out of his mouth.

"Tell him to get down from there. This is idiotic. He's going to fall off and break his neck," I said.

"He's all right."

"He is not."

"I can hear you, Mrs. Henshaw," said Pops. "And while I appreciate the concern, you can rest assured that I have undertaken this exercise many a time before. I once spent a night on a wire and got paid fifty dollars in the morning for it."

"You slept on a wire?" I said.

"That's good money," said Bud.

"Fifty dollars," said Pops. He spoke through pursed lips and had a look of concentration on his face. He was making the tips of his fingers flutter. There were huge sweat marks under his arms. A fly landed on his ear horn and then on the side of his face but he went on with his concentrating like it wasn't there.

"Now here it is, you all watching?" he asked.

"We're all watching, Pops," said Bud.

Pops said, "All right," then lifted up one of his legs and closed his eyes, then drew his arms into his chest and back out again, and when his fingertips were as far away from him as they could get he bowed his head, tensed the leg was on the tree branch, jumped, and landed on his other foot with a crash I thought would take down not just the branch but the tree entire.

"You can all start breathing again," Pops said, opening his eyes and smiling down at us. Which is when, like it was part of the trick, a big cornflower boy blowing on a whistle bloomed up out of the evening light. He was on a bicycle and had a referee whistle in his mouth and he was swooshing hard down the road as happy as a Baptist banging his Bible on the cash register. When he saw us he gave out a whistle or two, put on the brakes, and wobbled his way over the dusty gravel to a stop.

"It's a hot one," he said.

"Hot as they get," I said.

"Is this the road to Marvel? I was told it was."

"You heading there? Today of all days?"

"Could be. What's that feller doing up in that tree?"

"This is what I was doing," said Pops. He lifted his leg up again but our attention had turned elsewhere and his leg drooped back down.

"Listen, I'll give you ten dollar for that bicycle," Bud said.

The boy laughed and blew on his whistle.

"You'd buy a bicycle from a cornflower?" he said. "I thought this was cornflower-killing country. 'Today of all days.'" He looked at me when he said this. Gave out a handsome grin.

"If it would get me where I was going on a hot day, yes, I would," said Bud.

"Hell, I'll give you fifteen," said Dale.

"You ain't got fifteen," I said.

"Well, I'll give you what I got," said Dale.

"What you got is nothing since it's all in my purse or ate up by your pig," I said.

"He have a pig?" said the boy. "I like pigs. I got a grand-daddy works at a slaughterhouse.

"You have any pigs?" said the boy. He was looking at Bud. He hadn't turned his head, just his eyes.

"I'm in insurance," said Bud.

"Why don't you sell me a policy?"

"You have money?"

"I've got this bicycle."

Bud laughed. The boy didn't. He looked over at Dale without moving his head then back at Bud. He spoke slowly.

"Maybe you want to try to take my bicycle, mister," he said. He said it seriously but Bud took it like it was a joke.

"What if I did?"

"You think you could accomplish the task?"

"Listen to how this cornflower talks!"

"Do you think you could?"

"If I wanted to. 'Course I could."

"Why don't you, then?"

"Maybe I will."

"I had a bicycle once; she was a beaut, built just like a pretty lady," said Pops. Somehow or other he had got himself down out of the tree and come over to sit beside us. He had to cough in the middle of saying it and when he coughed he shook his ear horn off its kilter. The boy turned his head and his eyes both and smiled.

"You folks all done dropped your biscuits on this hot evening," he said.

Bud bristled a little when he said it but he didn't get up and it was a good thing, in my opinion, even for Bud, that the boy and his powerful legs was already swooshing away.

"I'd have taken that bicycle if I had wanted it," said Bud when he was gone.

"'Course you would have," said Pops. "We'd of helped you too. Wouldn't we have, Dale?"

Dale didn't say anything. Bud blustered about how he wouldn't have needed any help. Not against any cornflower kid wearing a whistle.

"I know you wouldn't have needed it. I'm just saying we would have helped you. That's different. It's two different things."

"I expect it is," said Bud. He looked over at me, no doubt in this world hoping I would offer up some additional puff about how he would have demolished that boy without even breaking any more sweat, but you could see Pops had already got the ship turned back straight enough. Bud was simple that way. I gave him a smile but kept my mouth shut.

"Anyways, a bicycle is a beautiful thing," said Pops. He said it soft and dreamy. As if bicycles had been as important to his past as being skinnier and sleeping on wires.

"The hell they are," said Dale. "You can crash on those things quicker than you can sneeze. And next time leave Sassy out of it, Ottie Lee."

That's what he called that pig. He had named her that spring to spite me. Lord in heaven. I don't think I need to say any more about it.

"I'm bored and hot. I want my rematch," I said.

"You ain't getting any rematch, Ottie Lee."

"Then I want a dance."

Dale clicked his tongue and shook his head.

"We'll hum. Or Pops can sing. You'll sing while we dance, won't you, Pops?"

"Sure I will," said Pops. "What'll it be? I can sing anything and climb trees both. You all saw that, didn't you? You saw me up in that tree? That boy stole my thunder. I used to do that on the wire. Anytime I wanted to."

Pops was already clearing his throat and priming his song pump, and I began to stand, but then Bud surprised us all by starting to cry. You couldn't tell what it was at first; it looked like he had his head down and was laughing.

"Now I have seen it all," said Dale.

"Leave him be," I said.

"He's thinking about them is what he's doing," Pops said.

"He's drunk too much is what it is," said Dale.

"Too much drink and too much sun," I said. "He'll be all right." I didn't know if he would be or wouldn't but it was something to say.

Bud cleared his throat and wiped his mouth. He gave us over a sorry smile and a drippy, half-assed laugh. "Memory lane, it just kind of came up on me, didn't even know I was driving down it, my girl had a bicycle," he said, his voice cracking a little. "A minute ago you were going to dance," he added, then his face crunched up and his shoulders gave a heave and he buried his head in his hands.

"You *were* going to dance with me, Dale Henshaw," I said.

Dale shrugged, looked at Bud, then at me. "You're the one never wants to dance."

I started to deny it, then stopped. I've already said it was true. Least the part about dancing he was referring to.

Pops walked over and gave Bud a pat on the back then followed it with a couple of sharp whacks. He said, "Let's get up and go. We got to go. We got to *git!*"

"Every goddamn thing is going to the show and here we sit," said Dale.

Not a one of us moved, though.

And even though Bud quit his crying soon enough and got back to joking and bragging, I don't think any of us even much more than looked up a little while later when a truck following its headlights went speeding past. Tell you what, we all got interested when that truck stopped. It took a while for the dust to settle but we didn't have to see much to know who it was.

"Ottie Lee and Dale and Bud and good old Pops!" Sally Gunner hollered out at us from the middle of her cloud of dust. She had on sturdy black work boots and a wore-out-looking yellow dress fit too tightly at the shoulders.

"Ho there, angel lady," said Bud.

"Hello, Bud!" said Sally. "You all want a ride?"

You can imagine about how long it took us to get into that vehicle, me up front next to Sally, the boys in the back on the truck planks, and a minute later we were running down the road as fast as you like.

"You come along just in time, we were getting wore out," I said.

"I just bet you were," Sally said.

I'd never ridden anywhere with her and I already told you

she took visits from angels, but she sure knew how to drive. That truck must have been built to help fight the kaiser but she ran it straight down the road like she'd got shot out of a cannon. She had strong arms, did Sally, and when the steering wheel tried to have its way she yanked it back straight like it was nothing.

Sally and I had been in school together. That was a long stretch before she got herself hit on the head and started having her breakfasts with the winged ones. In those days, she had been sharp as a tack with her letters and sums. After my father was done with trying to sell soaps and dishes and company shares and didn't need anyone to look after me for weeks and months at a time and I was done with the Spitzers forever, Sally and I had fallen in together and I'd played with her regular for a while. We jumped and wrestled and sang songs and caught frogs and even buttoned on the same kind of frocks a day or two and wore them to school. Then we grew up. Sally's father, who was better than half cornroot, had been a sheep hand on a big farm. He'd got himself killed in a herding accident but not before stacking some two-by-fours in the haymow where they could drop down on someone.

"This was my daddy's truck," Sally said.

The truck was old and didn't have any side windows and the boys in the back were probably holding on tight for their dear life, but now we'd get to Marvel. We'd get there and we'd get a spot and we'd see the show. It wouldn't just be Charley Goodwin and Candy Perkins and those bloodhounds who got to go. I'd get my message. I'd see my light. Light to chase the dark. To lead me on my way. And it was Sally carrying me there. Only when we came to the Marvel turnoff, which would have meant we didn't have more than a few miles left to go, she didn't take it, she just kept right on. I could hear one of the boys pounding on the back window but I reckoned Sally had thought out her own way to get to Marvel and I didn't ask her about it. One time before we'd gone our separate ways I'd played in the woods with Sally and felt lost and cried and cried for my mama who of course couldn't come, but Sally with her beautiful sharp nose had known how to get home like we weren't twelve-year-olds and hadn't wandered around in the gullies for hours and been about bit to death by bugs. True again, that was before she'd had her head half caved in by a two-by-four.

"Gonna be something," I said.

"Sure enough it is," she said.

"I'll bet half the whole world will be there."

"I do hope so."

"They was organizing buses out of Ryansville earlier."

"You don't say it?"

"How are those angels of yours?"

"Oh, they are fine, my goodness, yes."

"You don't think this is what they had in mind for me, do you? That special thing? The one Abraham Lincoln was talking about."

"It might be!"

"'Cause I could use some light, Sally."

"Couldn't we all!"

"And just think, it's you taking me, Sally. You getting me over the last stretch."

"I suppose it is!"

"You think you could ask them some more about it?"

"Oh my goodness, no, they never talk to me after my breakfast, Ottie Lee."

We went roaring down the road and after a while whoever it was quit banging on the back window and I thought my thoughts and swallowed down the doubt or two it was true I had about heading up to see a lynching, swallowed it straight down. I went far away off elsewhere with my thoughts, best I could, and Sally hummed, something sweet, and nothing like whistling, so that when we pulled up next to a line of cars in front of a little countryside meetinghouse it took me a minute to put it together that we hadn't just arrived in Marvel. Matter of fact, when we stopped I was so sure we were where we weren't that I yanked open my door, jumped outside, and said, "We're here!"

"Here where?" said Pops.

"That there is a Quaker meetinghouse, not a lynching tree," said Bud.

"You start talking to angels too while you was in there with her? We're halfway back the way we come!" said Dale.

They were each one of them covered up in road dust and Pops was holding his hip and giving out little groans.

Sally came around the truck about as cheerful as a flamingo found itself in fresh water and said, "I reckon they've got started, but that's all right, they'll go all night."

"Reckon who's started what?" I said.

"Well, come on in with me and see."

The boys looked daggers at both of us, but they followed over to the church just the same. As we rode, there at the end, I'd been getting myself ready for the riot in Marvel, for what I would see and how I would feel about it, and most of all what I would learn, so when we stepped in through the door and into that church, what we saw there came across as extra-strange. Like with those bloodhounds or Bud's bawling, it came up so cockeyed I didn't entirely understand what I was seeing. At first it looked like regular old bowed heads, what you might expect. Up near about a hundred of them. And not a one of them moving a twitch or pronouncing a word. Fair enough and nothing to write home to your friends and family about. Then I heard one of the boys behind me take in a hard breath and a second later I took in my own. I took it in because I'd just seen it too: the church was filled to its fat gizzards with cornsilk and cornflower folks both. Maybe even some cornroots besides Sally and corntassels too. All of them sitting next to each other like they was one great big shook salad in one great big salad bowl.

"What is this?" I whispered over to Sally.

"Prayer vigil."

"Prayer vigil why?"

"Against the hangings."

Sally said this and patted my arm then went and sat down and bowed her head next to a cornflower lady in a purple hat. As I watched, Sally gave that cornflower lady's hand a squeeze and that cornflower lady smiled and squeezed her hand back.

The world can shut your mouth for you sometimes. Get so big right there in front of you it won't fit into your eyes. The Spitzers had a well out back of their house a couple of the other kids there dangled me down into. They did it 'cause I'd told them to. Mr. Spitzer had said over supper that night he had seen the moon sleeping down in that well once and I wanted to see it. I didn't see any moon down there with the cold walls curdling all around me but funny thing was, before those other kids pulled me back up, I thought I heard it whisper at me. And what I thought I heard it whisper was "Surprise!" Mr. and Mrs. Spitzer both were waiting up top with switches for us and I never went back down that well and hadn't much considered it since but that was the first thing I thought of when I looked out over that congregation: dangling down a tunnel into a dark had deep water for its bottom. Water and something else. Something waiting. Something in the deep didn't yet have its name.

Not a one of us said a word as we walked away from that place of worship. We just walked and kept what we didn't have to say or didn't know how to say to ourselves. Cornsilks and cornflowers sitting there side by side. Heads bent and shoulders touching. A whole houseful. A few times as we went, one of the boys breathed heavy or kicked a rock off into the ditch but that was about it as far as the serenades go.

Which suited me fine. Let me dangle down a while longer over the dark water. Who doesn't like some quiet? At home the animals were always hollering, or Dale was grumbling, or the floorboards were shrieking like they was still trees in the forest being chopped down. In Bud's office there was always Bud snoring or Bud opening and shutting the window or Bud whooping because he had just made another sale or because someone had died the right way so he wouldn't have to honor their policy or Bud telling me to answer the phone. There *was* some crickets and katydids come up to saw away at the evening along with the birds and squirrels, but you can't call the evening sounds of the countryside loud. You get to walking— even with a sweat on you and the air too close for comfort and a long ways still to go and nary a wet drink to be had—and there ain't someone jawing at you, then you can start to hear the sound of your own breathing and the sound of your own steps and feel the swing of your own arms through the atmosphere.

I don't think when it's quiet. I don't recall. I don't bring back to mind, for example, Dale closing his magazine and asking the lady standing on our front porch in her heavy coat to come in. Come in and sit down and take a seat, even though it was as clear as the night was warm that everything about the stranger was wrong.

Still, who ever heard of a quiet that didn't come to a clatter about the time you were settling into it? Sure enough, it wasn't more than some short minutes after we had struck off on a shortcut Bud knew through a tired-looking bean field and down what was looking like a sleepy lane when we heard Sally Gunner calling on us to wait up.

"What in hell now?" said Dale.

"Comes the angel lady again," said Pops.

"Let's hurry up so she can't catch us," said Bud.

But she caught up with us, did Sally Gunner, caught up and fell right in.

"Meeting break up?" I said.

"No, they're still going, I told you they're just getting started," she said.

"But you come running along to see how we were, see how we were enjoying our walk," said Pops.

"Hell," said Dale.

"What happened to your truck?" I said.

"I promised it to some boys wanted to fetch some folks didn't have rides over to the prayer vigil."

Bud and Pops stopped dead when Sally said this. Then they shook their heads and spit. For his part Dale shot me over a look I didn't know how to read. Then they each one of them walked on.

"Well, we're shoe-soling it to Marvel," I said.

"I know," Sally said. "I just wanted to see how you were coming."

"We're coming."

"Sure you don't want to go back? Join us? Join in?"

"Lord Almighty, Sally. We're going to Marvel."

"You mind if I walk along with you a spell?"

Bud snorted.

I told Sally I didn't mind. I said I'd be just pleased as strawberry punch to have her stroll along through the evening with us. I told her we were having a grand old time walking all the way to Marvel especially after we had visited her fine vigil and wouldn't hardly miss her truck a bit. Walking, I told her and gave out a big grin, was a sweet exercise and it was pleasant in the rare extreme to do when you had good company.

"I agree, Ottie Lee. I completely agree," she said.

"Hell," Pops said.

Dale gave me over his look again but I still couldn't read it. I mouthed over *What?* at him but I knew as soon as I had done it that he would think of me and Bud mouthing back and forth at each other in the car and sure enough he gave me the stinkbug eye and stomped off.

The boys all three picked up their pace and walked ahead of us then so that after a while it was just me and Sally in the night. I jawed at her some more about the delights of two-footing and about how nice it was not to have to be riding in a fast truck to Marvel but she just sweetly smiled it all off. Once or twice I tried to set into something else tart to say about Abraham Lincoln and the angels but her smiles and nods and "I agree"s kind of wore me down. So we just walked. Feet and arms in smooth motion. Even our breathing come out about the same. I got it into my head that I wanted to tell her about the well and how the well had whispered "Surprise!" and how I had thought about that when I had seen her vigil, and so I told her, and she nodded and said it was a surprise, a wonderful surprise, for it was the future sitting there bowing its head.

And it was when she said this that something happened. It wasn't much of a something and it didn't last long but there we went a-swinging and for a dozen or two steps I felt just exactly like I had floated away from myself and down the dark well and through the water and up into Sally and that I was looking along the road out of her little eyes. Up ahead I could see Pops, Dale, and Bud, and off to my side, I could see Ottie Lee—heavy-chested lady in a green dress with a neat little nose, a wrinkle or two around the eyes, hair limp in the heat, and a scowl on her face. The evening kind of pillowed up around me when I was walking along like that. Being Sally. Not being me. My feet stopped hurting and I lost some of my hankering to get somewhere so fast.

"Why don't we slow down a step," I said. Only when I said it I was back over in my own self. Sally didn't answer so I scrunched my eyes a minute and when I opened them I'd gone again through the well water and was looking back out of her eyes and this time, though I hadn't noticed it before, I could see little points of light buzzing all around in the trees. They were pretty and I wanted to step off toward them but I knew I wasn't supposed to so I just kept walking my borrowed long legs and swinging my borrowed long arms and when another dozen or two steps were over, Sally spoke out of my mouth and said, "It's funny, everything looks different. Feels different too," and I spoke through Sally's mouth and said, "It surely does," and Sally said, "Well, I just wanted to walk awhile," and I said, "Stay on a minute," and Sally said, "I don't know," and I said, "Why not?" and she said, "I don't like where it is you all are going," and I said, "Where is it we're going?" and she said, "Aren't you all going to the lynching?" and I said, "That's the plan," and she said, "That's the wrong way," and I said, "It's wrong to go to a lynching?" and she said, "I think Bud's cute, he's awful cute," and I said, "But I am going, Sally, I am going to go," and she said, "Don't tell him, Ottie Lee," and I said, "Toward the torch of clarity, the beacon of Abraham Lincoln's bright light," and she said, "I couldn't stand it if you told him," and I said, "I need some clarity, I need to see something true," and she said, "Promise me you won't tell him," and I said, "Tell him what?" and she said, "He was nice to me once, I was so sorry to hear about his wife and daughter, especially his daughter, she was little bitty when she went," and I said, "He was crying about them earlier," and she said, "Bud Lancer was crying?" and I said, "Had to see it to believe it," and she said, "He has a tender heart," and I said, "You fetched along out here with your angels to talk about Bud?" and she said, "I never see my angels at night," and I said, "The hell," and she said, "Please don't curse, Ottie Lee, I got to get going now," and when she said

80

this I was back looking out my own eyes and breathing out my own nose and the little lights in the trees were gone and there wasn't anything to do except start thinking and remembering again and give out a spit and a shiver and watch Sally go.

"Where'd she get off to?" said Bud. He and the others had stopped to let me catch up. As soon as I had, they started walking again.

"Back to that church to pray, I reckon," I said.

"Church, hell," said Dale and belched.

"What were you trying to tell me a minute ago?"

"Wasn't trying to tell you anything."

"She thinks you're cute, Bud. She likes you," I said.

"Hell in a horse wagon she does."

"It might even be love."

"I think I done been struck by lightning and now I'm going to die and you can bury me by the river and sing a few songs," said Bud.

"Sally Gunner, the angel runner," I said.

Bud set in to running in circles and flapping his arms. He was a lot more fun when he was being stupid and not crying or bragging and I ran off after him doing the same.

"The two of you is scaring me now," said Dale.

"We're flying toward the future!" I said.

We flapped and fooled another minute then stopped and walked on laughing a nice while longer, then Pops stopped short and gave a low whistle. "Well, howdy, if it ain't some cornflowers with a wagon," he said.

There wasn't much of anything but moonlight to see by, but indeed there they were, four of them worrying away at a two-bench wagon stuck in a rut. We got up close and you could see it was three gals and a little old man. They all had on their Sunday best and when we come up out of the dark, the older of the three gals give out a shriek.

"Get behind me now," the man said to the gals. He had a deep voice despite his small size. They did as he said.

"Got your wagon stuck, did you?" said Bud.

The old man didn't answer and the women were shaking their heads and looking over at us and muttering. Every now and then their big mule stamped a foot and flicked its tail.

"Looks like they caught a rut," said Pops.

"You all got any water?" Dale said.

The old man pointed up at the wagon and Dale went over and fetched down a jug from the back. As he came back with it, a moth flew in front of his face and he gave a start.

"You're not going to drink out of that, are you?" said Bud.

"Hell if I ain't," Dale said. "You wanted to buy a cornflower bicycle before. Now you don't want to drink their water?"

"I'd of taken that bicycle if I'd wanted it," said Bud.

"I drunk with cornflower folks before," said Pops.

"Tastes just like water," Dale said, spilling a good amount of it down his throat.

"I'll try some of that if these folks don't mind," said Pops.

The old man nodded, slow and wary, and Pops sloshed some of the water out onto his face. He tried again and got some into his mouth. When he was done he handed me the jug and I got some down too. The old man looked back and forth between us. One of the women, didn't look to me like she had the brightest bulb burning in her head, had gotten down on her knees and clasped her hands. She was looking straight at me as she did so.

"You come over from Marvel?" asked Bud.

"Yes, we did, seems like it keeps catching up with us, though," said the man.

"They got the show going on over there yet? Tell us something about it," said Bud.

"Don't talk to them, Jasper," said the older woman.

"Jasper your name?" said Bud.

"Last I heard," said the old man. "I used it over in Europe when I wore the uniform. I use it on the papers to my house. People aren't friends and family call me by my last name, though, and generally attach a *Mister* to it."

"You folks heading over to the prayer meeting?"

The man didn't answer.

"One they was holding over in the little meetinghouse a mile or so up that way? We been there. It's going on right now."

The old man kind of squinted, then shrugged.

"Well, Jasper, this is your lucky evening and you may still make it because my friends and I here are going to help you get your wagon out of that rut."

The old man looked at Bud for a long time, then he nodded.

"We'd appreciate a speck of help," he said. "We took the corner too fast."

"I'll help anyone gave me water when I was thirsty," said Pops. "That's just Christian."

"Get on over here behind this wagon and give a push," said Bud.

So Bud, Dale, and Pops got behind the wagon and the old man took hold of the mule and when the old man said, "All right, now," to the mule, they gave a big push.

"Stuck good," said Bud, wiping his brow and giving out a little wheeze when the wagon had settled again.

"Yes, sir, it is," said the old man.

"But we ain't licked yet. You gals get on over here and give a hand."

The three women looked at the old man and I looked at them. A minute or two later we were all of us behind the wagon. As we got ready to push, the young one that had been on her knees fixed me hard in the eye again.

She said to me, "You shouldn't be doing this on a day like today. Not on any day."

"Helping you?" I said.

"None of it," she said. "You know they had a bloody shirt hanging out a window downtown?"

"I heard about that."

"It was all bloody. There were folks down in the crowd pointing up at it and laughing."

"Were you there? At the courthouse?"

"They'd of killed me if I'd gone down there."

"Well, I don't know why you're telling me this."

She didn't say anything else, just shook her head and shut her mouth, and thirty seconds later we had them unstuck.

"These girls got some muscle to them," said Bud.

The old man didn't waste any time and started to climb back up onto the wagon. Bud didn't waste any time either and put a hand on the old man's bird-bone shoulder. After pausing a few seconds, the old man stepped slowly back down.

"You folks were looking to get out of town and to the prayer meeting, were you?" said Bud.

"That's right," said the old man.

"Things a little testy over there in Marvel at the present time, I imagine," said Bud.

"Oh Lord, here we go," said the young woman who had spoken to me.

"You settle yourself down and keep your dignity," said the older woman.

"Well, no cause for alarm," said Bud, "but I expect you can reason out that us three here and the lady are fixing to catch the

85

show. No disrespect to law-abiding folks heading in the opposite direction to a mixed-participant prayer meeting like yourselves."

The old man said nothing. I could see Bud nod in the dark and hear him suck a little of the hot evening air in through his teeth.

"And that gives us a dilemma," he said, "since you folks have a fine wagon and due to circumstances beyond our control we are without appropriate or proper conveyance, and we have farther than you to go."

"Appropriate and proper is the same thing," I said.

"This is not our wagon," said the old man.

"Whose is it?" Pops said.

"We don't want any trouble," said the older woman. "There is plenty of trouble on this earth already tonight."

"Never said you did, ma'am," said Bud. "Did I say they did?" he asked Dale.

"No, you did not," said Dale.

"Lord come to us now," said the young woman.

"Get to your point, Bud," said Dale.

"My point?" he said. "Who says I have a point?"

"He wants the wagon, Grandpa," I said.

Bud cocked his head to the side and held up his hands. "I didn't hire her for nothing," he said.

Pops said, "This don't seem right. Does it seem right to you, Dale?"

Dale crossed his arms over his chest. "No," he said. "It does not."

"Then I say we let them get on their way."

"And I say let's let the lady decide," said Bud.

"Let Ottie Lee decide?" said Dale.

"Why not? She's got opinions on everything else."

They all turned and looked at me. The trembly young woman more than anyone else. Her and her Lord help us and bloody shirt and so on. Her and her *I* shouldn't be doing this. Like I shouldn't have done any part of my life. I paid those boys to dangle me down the well. Nickel apiece. I knew we'd all get whippings when I got back up. Earning whippings from the Spitzers was my specialty. My father used to say I was a chip off my mother's bad block. Once I put some bits of broken glass in his bottle. He drank them down and didn't die. We all do things. She was looking at me again, the trembly one. Because I was a woman. Jesus help us. And her lips were moving. Like it was me and the Lord both held the golden rope could yank them up out of all their problems.

"Let's take it," I said.

"You serious, Ottie Lee?" said Dale.

"I am," I said.

"She looks serious to me," said Bud.

"Lord almighty," said Pops.

"Now you sound like them," I said, my eye on the young woman, who had turned her thoughts back up into the air and wasn't looking my way anymore.

The old man didn't say a word, didn't even bother to spit again. The women didn't say another word either. They all four stood silent next to their water jug as Bud got the wagon turned, and they were silent as we loaded ourselves up and drove off. Some of that silence got carried up along on the empty parts of the wagon benches but after a minute the air got going around us and swept it away.

Pops whined and mumbled after we took the wagon and wouldn't sit up on the benches with us like we told him he should. He sat cross-legged in the back rocking this way and that and talking to himself loud enough for us all to hear. He talked about his church and his country and about Abraham Lincoln, of all things, just like that old man at Ryansville had. He talked about how he wasn't saying cornflowers wasn't cornflowers and cornsilks wasn't cornsilks but he had served in the war and seen cornflowers fresh up out of Africa battle the kaiser with their bare hands and American cornflowers stand up to fight when no one else would. Dale sat on the benches with us but made it clear he was on Pops's side of the affair. Going to a lynching of clear criminals was one thing, he said, but stealing a wagon and its mule from folks not bothering anyone was another.

"Borrowing," said Bud.

"Oh, that was borrowing, not stealing, excuse me, I misunderstood," said Dale.

Pops said that if he had been younger and didn't have his goiter he'd have stopped it but that he wasn't young and had his goiter. That goiter troubled him something pretty awful.

It was the devil's torment, pure and simple. Made it so he couldn't sleep most nights.

"I thought you had that goiter taken care of," said Bud.

"What?" said Pops.

"Even if I agree with you on the matter of principle, you ain't got a goiter anymore; been five years now is what he said," said Dale.

Pops snorted. He said even if his goiter was gone he was still troubled by it when he swallowed and no one ought to have taken a wagon and left folks trying to get to a prayer vigil to set in the dark by the side of the road.

"Dark's good for praying. I do my best praying after dark," said Bud.

"What praying do you ever do?" I said.

"I pray plenty," said Bud.

I started to say something else then thought of him sitting there bawling about his wife and daughter and kept it to myself.

Behind us Pops belched and this made Bud start to laugh but then he remembered that he didn't have anything to drink. "I'm thirsty," he said.

"Shoulda drunk some of that good cornflower water before you stole the wagon," Dale said.

"Wagon you're riding in, husband," I said to Dale.

"Not that kind of thirsty," Bud said. "Pops, you thirsty?" he called.

"What did you say?" said Pops.

"Did your hearing contraption stop working?"

"Works fine."

"Well, I said are you thirsty?"

"Could be."

"Could be or are?"

"I wouldn't say no to a sip," said Dale. "Even if what happened back there was wrong."

"No one said you had to climb up and ride," I said.

"Oh, you think I should have stayed back there with them?"

"I'm just saying you had a choice. We all had a choice."

"Yes, we did. Every one of us." Dale looked long at me when he said this.

I looked back and said, "Are we going to Marvel or aren't we?"

"Maybe this piece of hocus-pocus will show us the way." Bud had the reins in his lap and his hands on what I leaned over and thought first was a painting then saw was some kind of a map. It had been rolled up and was now curled in at its four bent edges. Bud said he had found it on the wagon floor.

"Looks like I might have mussed it some. It's got symbols and markings on it. And all those pictures. Look at that. I'm surprised there aren't witches and brooms."

I told him to hand it over to me so he could drive and I could get a look and he said he didn't want to be holding it anyway and gave it straight over. Dale leaned in close for a look too. Pops kept to himself in the back and grumbled. It was handmade, no doubting that. Done on something like butcher paper. Had little pictures of cornflowers and corn-roots pasted all around its edges. Pictures cut out of news-papers and magazines and pasted on careful. It was decorated all over the rest of it with shiny green and gold and red and blue and silver and purple and black paint. I thought maybe there was more colors hiding on it but you couldn't see it that well.

"Is there a lantern on this wagon?" I asked.

"Lantern, hell," Bud said.

Dale pulled a box of matches out of his pocket and struck one on the wagon seat.

He held it cupped and close, and my eyes went around the paper's edge, first around the frame of photographs, little faces stern and smiling both, then around the next area where it had *North, East, West,* and so on painted in a pretty hand and each its own color. There was some towns scattered deeper in like Carlsboro and Oil City and Cherryton and Margaretville. But there weren't any roads or lanes marked. The damnedest thing. Just the river, a twisting black ribbon across the whole of it. The first match went out and Dale struck another and I leaned in again and saw there were black dots speckled here and there next to the towns and not next to them. Dale tapped at a couple of these dots with the little finger of his match hand and I told him to quit and he told me he would tap on it if he goddamn well pleased.

"That's the spirit," Bud said.

"Mind your own, Bud," I said back.

Bud said something about how it was him had found the nasty thing and he would say what he wanted and take it back too, all of which I ignored, while Dale gave the map one more big tap, right at its middle. At that middle was another photograph, of a courthouse, and under it was the word *Marvel* painted in purple letters. The match Dale was holding went out and when it did he turned away to spit over the side of the wagon, but he also lit another match and held it out to the side for me while he pretended to look out at the countryside. The little flame flickered so I grabbed his wrist and guided it where I wanted. Cupped it and leaned in close. I leaned in and took a good hard gulp of breath and held it because now I could see what I hadn't first seen, which was that there was silvery lines heading back and forth across the middle of the page. They went from one black dot to another and they all met up at Marvel. The longer I looked the smarter the silvery lines shined up. Looked like a fierce-headed blazon shining bright, just like I had been seeing it all afternoon, and here it was pouring even just out of a piece of paper, even just out of a name.

"Marvel's all lit up on this map!" I said.

"Map of what, though, is what I'm wondering and who in hell are all those cornflowers," said Dale, who had quit his considerations of the dark and lit another match and turned back.

"There's cornroots there too and it's the countryside," I

whispered, suddenly feeling small as a girl down a well. "It's right here. It's all around us."

"That's some cornflower magic-making, I'm telling you," Bud said. "They're looking to magic Marvel down. Head off the lynching. Set those boys free and who knows what all. 'Course, it won't work here in God's country. Lord, I'd toss that thing."

"Those were Christian people, not any kind of magic-makers," Pops called up from the back.

"It's just a map. Someone's map." My voice was back to snapping strong again. "I wish I knew what it was for."

"It's a map about those black dots. Those lines go from dot to dot," Dale said.

It was true. The silvery lines weren't coming out of Marvel; they were cutting straight through. Didn't make it shine up for me any the less.

"Makes me think about the underground railroads they had around here. Did you know they had the rails running all around here?"

"Everyone knows that and I'm telling you, that's a spell-caster's map. Burn it would be best. Set your match to it, Dale."

"It's a painting, pure and simple, is what it is. It's like art. Whoever made it had a good hand. I'd put it on my wall. We ought to bring it back to the folks it belongs to. Along with this wagon," said Pops, who had leaned up close enough to look over my shoulder.

"Why's a map got to be *for* anything?" I said.

"It's for getting somewhere or it's not a map. Lend me one of those matches, friend Dale, and I'll burn it," said Bud.

"That's just jackass talk," said Pops.

"You want to say that again?" said Bud.

"Hee-haw!" said Pops.

"No one's burning anything," I said, rolling the paper back up and shoving it down on the seat between me and Dale.

"Anyway, I know a place just up the road," said Bud after he had cast a glance or two over his shoulder at Pops, who had gone back to his spot.

I gazed up the lane. While we had been studying the map, the moon had taken a cloud and the countryside had gone about pitch-black and I couldn't see a thing.

"Like that store you knew about earlier," I said.

"Well, maybe my spot is on that map of yours, why don't you check? Let it lead the way."

"I thought it was your map."

"I don't want it."

"You can give it back when you return this wagon you borrowed. Just like Pops suggested," said Dale.

Bud spit and clicked his tongue. "A good old boy keeps a still in his shed. Just up over there yonder. He'll sell us a jar."

So the mule trotted on and the wagon bumped down the dark lane and a half mile later we took a turn and the turn took us to a house ought to have been, speaking of burning, torched off the earth a long time ago. There was a man on the porch of this house sitting on a swing under a lantern and in his hands he held a piece of rope. When we drove up he held up his piece of rope and gave out a whoop. Bud whooped back.

"Going to be a lynching up the road!" said the man.

"Where we're heading, by God!" said Bud.

"But you got thirsty on the way and come to see me," said the man.

"Yessiree," said Pops, who somehow or other had found his way without my knowing it back up onto the bench beside Dale.

"Well, come on down from the wagon and I'll line you boys up. Lady too if she likes it."

The man pushed up off the swing and grabbed a crutch and you could see that he was missing a foot.

"Farming accident," whispered Bud. "He's got a wife somewhere around here if she ain't dead."

The man was so filthy he looked like he'd rolled around in bacon grease then taken a long nap under the tail of a sick cow. He led us back to a shed out in some high grass behind his rotting house. The shed wasn't in much better shape. It had developed a lean and about the only thing keeping it from falling over on its side was a shrub mulberry grown all out of control. My father had had a shed about like this out back of the house where he had gone to heave or howl and beat his sorry head against the walls.

"I hear them Marvel cornflowers dishonored twenty-five women," the man said as he crutched ahead of us.

"What I heard too," said Bud.

The man hadn't let go of his piece of rope and when he spoke he waved the end of it around. The end was frayed and wet-looking, like he had been chewing on it. I expect he had. He had a rusty still in a corner of the shed and a row of mason jars filled with cloudy hooch.

"I'm giving out a show-day discount to any who buys two."

"I'm in," said Pops.

"Two'll do," said Bud.

"Give him my money, Ottie Lee," said Dale.

"Ottie Lee?" said the man, looking up at me.

"Ottie Lee done scraped her knee," I said, rolling my eyes.

They all laughed loud enough to bring the shed down. As a matter of fact, thinking this choice thought, I stepped outside while they were still chortling and taking their first drinks and leaned against the side of the shed and pushed out hard as I could with my legs but alas on me, the rotten structure held. They always do. So I left them to their chortling and went back around to the front of the house and retrieved the map and got myself settled next to the mule.

I talked to the mule awhile but the mule fell asleep while I was addressing it. I let this bother me some for a minute and accordingly gave the beast a whack or two with the map on its meaty flanks but it didn't wake. There had been a mule liked to lounge along the other side of the fencerow at the Spitzers' and I had visited it a good deal. Remembering this—remembering going out to see it after I'd been whipped or some such for forgetting to comb my hair or wetting my bed or singing too loud or singing too low or leaving dirty dishes or getting the others to do my work for me—I laid my head on that sleeping mule's meaty shoulder and spoke to it. I spoke to it about this and about that. I spoke to it about what I still planned to say to Candy Perkins when I saw her at the show. I spoke to it about that big fat Sassy pig of Dale's and how I couldn't hardly wait until she was bacon and we could have the money she brought and I could tell Bud and his bonuses to go to hell. I spoke to it about those idiots out there drinking in the shed. I unrolled the map and moved my eyes around it as I spoke, went from face to face, let my eyes ride along the silvery lines, skitter across its surface, and land on its other side. In the light coming off the house I could see the black dots were rectangles. I counted twenty-six of them. The silvery lines had been painted straight as sharp-pulled thread. I turned the map this way and that as I looked, and as it moved in the light, it sparked and shone. So I spoke to the mule about those bright specks I'd seen as I walked along thinking I was looking out of Sally Gunner's angel-runner eyes. How I thought I had seen them again the minute before I hadn't told Bud we shouldn't steal from those poor corn-flowers. I told the mule maybe I had seen those lights and maybe I hadn't. But here I was looking at that map and maybe seeing them again. "I'm looking for my Pearl," had said the woman in her overcoat sitting in my chair in the front room. She had looked very slowly over at me when she said it. She had no teeth, false or real. She could have been forty or a hundred. There must have been a light rain come up because there was water dripping off her heavy coat and the water drops on the wood floor glittered and shone.

I didn't make much out of the map beyond my own thoughts and memories but I spoke to the mule for a good while. Every now and again it would flick its ear at something that was troubling its mule dreams. As a girl paying my calls on the mule by the Spitzers', I had wished I had ears that could flick. Legs that could gallop. Hooves that could kick. I asked the mule I was leaning against if it knew what the map meant. Just a hint would do. I was ready for a clear road, I told it. That was when I heard the door open on the old house.

"They'll be at it all night if he gets his way with them." It was an ancient woman, a not much cleaner counterpart to the cripple entertaining the boys out back.

"I expect," I said.

"I know," she said. "Boys are out here every night of the week and he knows how to keep them going. Right now he'll be showing them how to tie a noose."

"A noose?"

"He knows all the knots."

"Well, then, he ought to be over at Marvel."

"Maybe so, maybe so." The woman had sat down a minute on the porch swing but now she stood up again and leaned back against the front door. "But I'll tell you what," she said, "he ain't going nowhere tonight."

"Is that a fact?"

"Like I'd carved it in stone."

"Like you'd chopped it out with a chisel."

"Hit it hard with a hammer."

"Sewed it up with some thick thread."

We had a laugh together and then we both settled down.

"What's that you're studying?"

"Nothing."

"Well, that's some shiny nothing, leastways that's how it looks from over here."

"It's colorful anyway," I said. "It came with the wagon. It's a map. Well, some kind of a map."

"Ain't that your wagon?"

"We borrowed it. For the evening. To get us to Marvel." As I said it, I rolled up the map and put it on the bench. Then, afraid some breeze might blow it or some night bird might steal it, I set it down on the wagon floor.

"You don't need a map to get to Marvel."

"You'd think, wouldn't you? It's taking us a while."

"Which one of them are you with? Fellow had the reins?"

"What makes you think I'm with any of them?"

"You're with one of them."

"Did you just wink when you said that?"

"I won't deny it."

"The little one with the yellow hair."

The old woman looked at her nails, smiled at something about them or about me standing out in her yard looking more jackass than the mule.

"I'd of guessed the big one driving the wagon," she said, "that's some piece of fellow. I'd like to have me some of that beef stacked up over there yonder in my icebox."

I kind of cocked my head but didn't say anything. The old woman said, "Come on over here so I can get a better look at you."

"What for?"

She had pushed herself off the front door and come forward. She wore glasses and a pink frock. Or pink was what color it was supposed to be.

"You see that sign," she said, pointing up at the eaves.

I hadn't seen it before but there was a sign, hanging by one nail, behind a mess of half-dead ivy.

GOODY'S BEAUTY PARLOR, the sign read.

I shuddered a little.

"Step on forward," said the old woman.

"Are you Goody?" I said.

"No," she said. "I bought the sign from her."

"That's a old sign."

"I still keep my hand in. I retired a while back but I still got clients in the neighborhood."

"You cut hair?" I said.

"Cut, comb, and curl. You need some attention," she said. "You need some freshening up. A woman gets to a certain age and the whole shop starts to sag."

"I ain't that old," I said.

"You ain't that young either."

Whether she was onto something or she wasn't I didn't like hearing it. Still, I put a finger to my head, moved it around under my hat. It felt like my scalp was about to start sprouting mushrooms.

"You heading to the show, you don't want to walk in like that," she said. "The whole wide world will be there to see them boys strung up and you want to look according. Anyone who's anyone going to be there. Lord, the governor, for all you know."

I thought a minute. What I thought of was those bloodhounds with neckties on.

"I keep the parlor all ready to go; we can step right in," she said.

I must of peeked up at her own hair, which looked like plain old road tar poured out of a bucket, combed a little, and painted gray, because she said to me that she didn't care to use her talents on herself, only turned them outward, offered them unto others, thought of it as her sacred mission.

"They'll be coming back around soon," I said.

She came down the steps, crossed the yard, took my arm. "They're still at it," she said. "Don't you worry, they'll be at it for a good long while."

The parlor was the first room in the house and it looked like it had been soaked in water then spread with mayonnaise and left to turn. There was mold and dust and lumps and sags and strips of flypaper blackened up with flies. There was some pictures of presidents tacked up to the walls and an old stereoscope with a bent picture holder lying in a corner next to a spilled box of its cards on the floor. The swivel chair had cracked its leather many a year before, but I was worn out to the bone and the thought of plunking down a minute was a happy one. I unpinned my hat and set it on a counter next to a pickle jar. The jar had some good fat pickles in it and when I'd got myself settled into the chair, my hostess offered me one. I was more hungry than I'd thought about and before I knew it I'd thrown the whole thing down the hatch. She held the jar out again and, when I shook my head, took one for herself.

"I got a cellar full," she said. "Secret to my longevity. That old thing out on its crutch won't touch a pickle. Says they give him the hives. They might too."

She cackled a little about this then told me where he claimed to get them, his hives. Her sharing this location didn't help the pickle I'd swallowed settle down any too gently and I wasn't sorry when she set the jar aside and looked to my hair.

You can say what you like, but mold on the premises or no mold, there isn't much else like some fingers know their business working at your head. The old woman pulled out combs and brushes and scissors and clippers. Lined them up neat between my hat and the pickle jar. Said she'd put my mess all straight. Said there was nothing to set you up for an evening in Marvel town like getting your hair fixed.

"You'll be winning beauty pageants when I'm done. You got some head of hair on you, I'll say that," she said and clucked her tongue.

I didn't tell her this but I had as a matter of indisputable fact won a beauty pageant back in my time. I'd have been about a junior in high school. Living with my father. They'd had a little stage set up next to an exhibition tent at the town fair. We stood and danced and shimmied and jiggled on the stage for about three weeks it felt like, then the judges cast their votes. Candy Perkins had been on that stage with me. About every chance she had as we did our gyrations she told me my chest was too saggy or my arms were too long or my legs were too soft. I gave back as good as I got and knew there wasn't anyone in that tent, including Candy, could take their eyes off my hair, but even so, just to make sure she was clear on the score, after I'd got my crown I went straight off into the field with the boy she was sweet on. After we had got

105

ourselves good and dirty, he told me his name was Dale. He was older than he looked. He'd come into a spread had a big mortgage on it but it had potential. He told me he'd always thought, seeing me around, I was awful pretty but hadn't ever dared talk to me before. Well, we've talked now, I told him. Seeing Candy Perkins's face after we come back out of the field holding hands had been awful pleasant. I know it's not nice to say that, but I'm saying it. They'd given her a dingy sash to wear said RUNNER-UP.

It was hot in the parlor and the old lady hummed a tune like Sally had while she worked and by and by I left off thinking about beauty contests and Candy Perkins and started in to drift. I don't know if you ever drifted when you were riding across the countryside in a vehicle and even though you are dreaming it seems like you never shut your eyes. I have it happen to me here sometimes and that's what happened to me in that chair. I was asleep but my shut eyes kept looking out at the old lady's beauty parlor, at her fly-worried windows, at her row of bottles and brushes and crusty jars. The stereoscope was sitting on the counter now. It had been restored and had a card loaded up to be looked at but I couldn't tell which one. While I was sleeping like this and feeling like I was still awake, the old lady, or the version of her was in my head, told me a story.

"Once upon a time in the old days before you and me, and way out in the hinterlands, there was a man." She sighed once and then continued. "He had two daughters by a slave and he kept the two daughters to do his work after the slave died. Then he got married to a girl not much older than the daughters. The girl didn't give him any children but he worked on it every night just the same. When he got tired of the girl he started in on the daughters. The girl saw this and instead of helping the daughters she got jealous and made it harder on them. She gave them extra work and whipped them when they stepped wrong. Then one morning the man came up dead with a pigsticker in his neck and the daughters set the girl to work. They worked her all day and set a shackle to her at night. One of the daughters had found herself pregnant before the man had got himself his pigsticker present and she blew up like a balloon all those months they kept the girl at work. The pregnant one would sit outside the shed where they kept the girl shackled and sing at her stomach: *That's the way of the world, baby child, that's the way of the world.* Then one day the weather turned fair and the daughters both walked off."

"What happened to the girl?" I said. My voice in the dream sounded flat, like it was far off or someone else's.

"No one knows," the old woman said.

"What happened to the daughters?"

"No one knows."

"What about the child?"

"No one knows."

"Should I go up to Marvel and see the show? I got a map now. Sally Gunner said no."

" 'Course you should."

"But it's wrong."

"Wrong is the way of the world. Didn't you know that? Take a look at your map if you don't believe me, Ottie Lee."

I woke then. The old woman was standing next to me, humming, working her combs and clippers on my wet hair. The broken stereoscope was back on the floor with its box of spilled cards. I stood, ran into the yard, and heaved up her pickle and what was left of the catfish and the slaw and the two slices of peach pie.

"Come on back in, I ain't finished," she called when I'd stood up.

"I'm done," I said.

I swallowed hard, wiped my mouth and face, ran to the shed, and found the boys standing around the old man, who had a noose tied to his crutch. He had the long end of the rope thrown over a ceiling beam and was pulling the crutch up into the air like a puppet.

"We got to go, it's getting late," I said.

"So it is," Bud said.

"We don't want to miss the show," said Pops.

"Hell no, we don't," said Dale.

So those two had changed some of their tune. Drink and a late hour will do that.

"I'll just set out here a while longer," said the old man, looking up at his crutch with a grin on his face. The old woman was standing in the middle of the front yard with her hands on her hips. I reached into my purse and pulled out a dollar, but she just folded her arms over her chest and turned her head to the side. First thing I did when I was back up on the wagon bench was reach down and grab at the map and clutch it to my chest.

"What happened to your hat?" Dale said as we rode away.

"Never you mind. Never you mind at all."

Dale nodded and, smart fellow that he was, didn't say another word. I had expected to have a posse of dead drunks on my hand after all the time the boys had spent with the old man but if anything they looked a good sight better than when they had went in. The mule too looked the better for its nap and after we had bobbed along a while it hit me that whether or not that old lady had fed me a bad pickle or made her way into my dreams and ginned up a story to steal away my heart, I was feeling better than I had since we had started out. Mrs. Spitzer had always preached the virtues of a good purgative. And it was the one piece of her advice I had carried off when my father had taken me away that last time. In fact, I had taken it as we had ridden down one bumpy road after another, my father's cigar smoke slithering its way down my nostrils, though he did not appreciate it when I splattered both his shoes. I had felt better, though, after I had purged in that car of his and I felt better now. Maybe purging was all I needed. Carve the lamb chop out of the chicken. The turkey out of the tomato. The bean out of the corn. The coffin out of the pig. Never mind that there are some things can't be carved out.

You would have thought we would have reached Ohio by that time of the night but there were still a few last miles lay before us. I knew they had probably gotten started on their business over at Marvel, but the idea of almost being there in all that bright light to help me see forward, whatever else it was we would find, made the pill that we had missed something easier to swallow down. I had the map now. I'd seen where it meant for us to go. For all of us to go. Marvel and its marvels. There was the stringing-up and then there was all the rest of it. Who knew what fearsome wonders would populate the night; who knew how long it would all go on?

The mule went clippity-clop and pulled us across the dark earth. Every now and then a bat or big moth would come close and I would miss my hat. But it wasn't time for thinking of hats now. The outskirts of Marvel were approaching. There was business at hand. We had to be like those bloodhounds. The boys had the feeling too. Once in a while they would take a sip from one of the jars they'd gotten at the old man's, but it was just smart little sips, the kind to keep your courage up. Maybe that old man had talked some sense into them with his rope and his crutch. You could see they knew we were coming up on Marvel and that it wasn't the time anymore for fooling around.

Riding along behind that mule in that dark, going where we were going, I thought about the map and got the fancy idea that we were a ship crossing the waters, that we were captains on the high seas. The boys didn't say it, but I could see they had sat up straighter and were keeping a sharp eye out for when we would make land. I decided as our mule boat took us across the deep waters of the Indiana night that even chaw-cheeked as he was, old Dale had some noble line to his jaw, some slick purpose to the cast of his eye. I liked looking at him and thinking that kind of thought. He even gandered back at me once or twice and I could tell he liked what he saw. Which was me. That's all it was. Ottie Lee Henshaw. Married to little Dale Henshaw, who she had met one happy day in a cornfield. There were surprises everywhere. Not just down dark wells, not just in countryside churches. To hell with Bud Lancer and his groping and his big dumb broken-down car. I'd quit my job the next day and stay home and help Dale. We'd get the farm squared away right. Let that fat Sassy win us a prize. Pay down the mortgage and buy some more land and put it under cultivation. Maybe we'd travel. Get down to Indianapolis. Even make it to Kentucky. It wasn't just juggling and turkey suppers there. I'd heard they had caves in those parts that were ten miles deep. You could take a boat down there along streams they had underground and see special kinds of fish didn't have any eyes.

Maybe see an angel. Find some light. Find the moon in its sleep. Forget about lynchings. Long walks in the heat. Forget about autumn-night visits from toothless ladies. Get deep down dark into the earth and forget it all. Forget enough.

It was with that notion in my mind that I climbed down off the wagon to pay a visit to the bushes. The boys got the idea they all needed the bushes too so I stepped a good way down the road to keep myself clear of them. It might have been dark as grave dirt, but it doesn't take much to disturb you in your private pastimes. Which is why when I heard a kind of cough couldn't have been fifteen feet away I jumped up and back out of my squat and dropped the map I had been holding tight and landed my foot badly against a root and fell down and pulled up my undershorts. "Shit goddamn," I said. It took me a minute to find the map in the dark. I was ready to say a good deal more and begin to lay about me with my feet and free fist if I hadn't caught sight of who it was had done his coughing at me. He was lying in the middle of the quiet road, flat on his back, but not entirely blended into the pale gravel because of the color of his suit.

"I am gazing at the stars and intended no interruption," said the speechmaker. "The cough was meant to express as much."

"You could have coughed before I got started," I said.

"I'll confess to you that I had dozed. The minute and most delicate sounds you made woke me. I have ever been a light sleeper. In my schoolboy years my mother and father used to run half a mile down to the road when they wished to parley after my bedtime hour."

"I do not know the word *parley*," I said. I had come over closer to him. I had thought he might sit up now that he had announced himself but he didn't.

"Fish a little, you will find it."

I fished a little and found it. It was not the most unhandsome word I'd heard that evening.

"It derives from the Cajun. I heard it said all the time when I made my visits to New Orleans."

"You've been all the way down there?"

"And farther, madam."

"You don't need to *madam* me."

"I assure you, it is my deepest pleasure to accord you the respect it does seem to me you so well deserve."

"Anyways," I said. "What in hell?"

"My presence must intrigue you, madam. It intrigues me too. I cannot easily account for it."

"I figured you for a man in the front row of the festivities. Sitting surrounded by your brethren from the buses. Getting bathed in all that beautiful light."

"What light?"

"From the torch of clarity. You said that yourself."

"So I did, and the image pleases, but figure, madam, that instead of taking that bath of bold light, I have been lying here on the road for some time imagining you reclining in the dappled moon shade of one of the trees."

"I don't believe that for a minute," I said with a snort, just a small one.

"Ah, but the beautiful thing about it is you don't have to believe it or not believe it. It is a part of the universe and part of this night and will never leave it now."

"We're all drunk," I said. "We haven't got over there yet and we lost our car. We got a wagon now, though. It came with a map. This one right here. I had my hair fixed. In a beauty parlor. Well, some."

"A map, you say."

I waved it around. I couldn't tell if he saw me doing it.

"I have not had a drop this night," he said. "My faculties are alert, my vision unimpaired. I have my good legs and a sound heart, but I have not yet made it to Marvel either."

"This map is a map to Marvel. We can't miss it now."

"I don't believe in maps."

"What does that mean?"

He put his hand on his sound heart like that was his answer and I thought maybe he was being romantic after all his complimenting, but it was too dark to tell so I let it go.

"What happened to the buses?"

"Ah," he said. "The buses..."

He got quiet and the quiet was a long and shuffly one and as it went on I had a crazy idea spring into my head.

"Tell you what, you want to dance?" I said.

"Dance, you say?" he said.

He looked confused and I could understand why but didn't

114

know how to explain it to him. I thought he was fixing to clam up and start in to shuffling again but then he jumped up off the ground and made me a bow, one hand on his stomach, one on his back. Then he took his hand off his stomach and held it out to me.

"I do, madam," he said.

"You don't care that we don't have any music?"

"We don't need music. Why should we? We have the music of the night, of the spheres."

I took his hand with the one wasn't holding the map and he gave another little bow, then twirled me over to him and took me in his sweaty arms. Up and down the gravel we went. He moved like he had been made in a music factory; everything about him was creamy and smooth.

"I've been wanting to dance half the day," I said into his ear.

"As have I, madam, as have I."

"Do you think it's bad to want to dance?"

"I do not."

"Sometimes I want to just dance."

"It is a natural inclination."

"We have a Victrola at home. My husband hired himself out every Saturday for a year to pay for it."

"They are lovely machines."

We danced across the dust and gravel, sending up small clouds and giving it all some good scrape and crunch as we went, and with each twist and twirl I felt my dress lift and my

115

legs cool. We danced what could have been two minutes or an hour and then he let go of my hand and bowed at me again. After which he plunked himself straight back down onto the road and sat there cornroot-style and I joined him.

"I needed that, as I hope you did too," he said.

"I surely did," I said.

"Have you ever seen a lynching?" he said.

"I never have."

"I have had quite an adventure this afternoon and night but I expect it is nothing like being lynched."

"I expect not."

"I was threatened with tar and with feathers by more than one of my pursuers but managed to extricate myself."

"Tar and feathers!"

He shook his head. Lifted up a hand, then let it crumple and fall again.

"Well, now here you are."

"Here I am." He sniffed. "Have you ever had to extricate yourself from a delicate situation, madam?"

"No. Not extricate. Not exactly. You wouldn't call it that."

He leaned in a little toward me. He had a buttery-soft look on his face.

"It's just I managed not to die a time or two when I was little," I said.

"Not to die?"

"Not to get killed. There was a someone involved. But it was a long time ago. Long, long time."

"I'm very sorry."

"I am too."

After I said this he made his way flat onto his back again and I stretched myself out beside him. The road gravel was packed down tight, probably from our dancing, and wasn't any too hard on my back. There was all the warmth of the day rising out of it and it eased up some of the angry sensation in my legs and back. He had spoken out about stars but I couldn't see any. There was a haze to the night. All of it spun a little before my eyes after our dancing. And my drinking. And purging. And talking. Oh, my talking. I suddenly felt more tired than I had in years and if I hadn't slept just recently at the beauty parlor I might have allowed myself a light doze.

Instead, though, I just lay there with the map in my hand next to the speechmaker, who had his hair on straight and smelled not all that bad of sweat and flower water, and let the world spin and spin.

Spin like the record that was on the Victrola when the woman came in off the front porch and took the seat she had been pointed to and sat there with her shoes clanked hard to the floor like pieces of old iron. She was holding a small paper bag. It took her putting it prim on her lap and resting her hands on top of it as she sat there for me to understand that it was her purse. Her face skin was weather-beat. Her lips sunk where her teeth were gone. Her hat had some mesh on the front that had got snagged, a few stray berries that should have been a bunch. I did not move at first when the woman asked after her Pearl. The Victrola was spinning a waltz and I had been listening and thinking maybe Dale and I would take a turn and waltz our way into the bedroom. We'd been talking about how maybe now it was time. Do our part. Populate the earth, set some pups loose to frolic. Then Dale opened the door and the woman sat down with her paper bag and asked after Pearl and I had a bell go off in the back of my head, only it wasn't just like a bell, it was also like a burning. I did not look up. I had a cup of coffee and the newspaper spread out on the table in front of me. Dale had his robot-and-rocket-ship magazine. We had been picking at Red

Hot candies in a bowl. It was just a small burning, but a flame all the same. So it was only when Dale said, "That's my wife, Ottie, right there, there isn't any Pearl here, is there something we can help you with?," that I looked up.

"Ottie," said the woman. She had her eyes on Dale. "I was looking for my Pearl," she said.

She said this and the place in the back of my head burned hotter and part of me stood straight up out of myself and walked over and sat down on the floor next to her chair and put my head in her lap. I lay my head down and looked up at her and saw there was more than a chance she hadn't been bad-looking once. Like the woman in the picture my father had kept at the back of his shirt drawer. My father who had told me, when I was old enough to ask about her, that she was gone, then that she was dead, then that he had stolen me away, then, not too long before he died, that she had been incarcerated for trying, two times, when I was little, to put an end to me.

"They let you out," I said as I lay there with my head in her lap.

"I've been good," she said.

One of her hands came off her paper-bag purse and stroked gentle at my hair. The bell in the back of my head rang and burned both.

"I'm looking for my Pearl," she said.

"You know any Pearls?" said Dale to me.

"Yes, I do," I said.

Only it was the me lying with my head in my mother's lap that said it. The me sitting at the table—the me that hadn't moved—told Dale he had to see the lady out, that she had to go, that she had to be gone, that I was going to scream.

"Ottie," said the woman as Dale led her out. "Ottie Lee was the name of his mother."

"Whose mother?" said Dale as he saw her out to the porch, the Victrola done playing but still spinning, and walked her down the front path and out to the road, where he put her in his truck and drove her all the way, he told me when he got back, into town.

"You want to talk on this now or later?" he asked me when we were back at our spots, him in his chair but not reading his magazine anymore and me at the table holding the back of my head.

A week later there was a letter, postmarked Gary but with no return address, came in the mail with my name on it in neat writing: *Mrs. Ottie Henshaw.* When a week after that I opened it, I found a half-piece of rose-colored penny paper that said only *It's dark out here.*

We lay there quiet. There was rustlings in the trees and some crickets chirruping but otherwise it was just us. There was a nice-size part of me could have kept on lying there a week and another part feeling the gravel—even smooth as we had made it—getting to be sharp against my back. I was set to come to some kind of a decision when the speechmaker said, "Madam, I have been more casual with you than I ought to have been. It is an inner failing and all my own. I apologize. It was a liberty I feel the moral pain of to engage you in dance. You please me greatly, but I am reeling from personal and professional setbacks at the moment and, further, I am spoken for."

"Well, if it comes to that, I'm spoken for too," I said.

"Even if I did like that dance."

"I'll never forget it."

"Then we understand each other."

He found my hand and gave it a squeeze. Those fine fingers of his. It was right then as I was squeezing them back that the boys started hollering for me to hurry it up.

I gave out a good sigh. "You're going to have to join up forces with us," I said.

"Will the others welcome me?" he said.

"Hell with them if they don't."

"Can you help me up?"

"Can you help *me?*"

We neither one of us could help the other and finally it was Pops appeared and called out to Bud and Dale that the speechmaker from Ryansville was on the ground.

"I'm down too," I said.

But it was the speechmaker that the boys fussed over and pulled up and smoothed down and steered along the road and helped up into the wagon, leaving me to heave myself erect alone. I accomplished the task but only because Dale called out at me with a cackle anyone could have told meant he'd been at his jar some more that I needed to pick my ass up or get it drove over. When I got to the wagon, though, Dale was waiting there ready to help me up and the speechmaker had one of his pretty hands out and Pops and Bud were bowing and grinning like I was a noble lady and they were servant men and all I could bring myself to do was tuck the map in close to my chest and shove them out of the way and hop up a little faster than probably I should have and take my place on the driver's bench.

It took them a while to stop the playacting and calm down, with the speechmaker talking about what a fine wagon we had in our possession and what a fine, fine mule. "Aren't you a good boy," he said, and the mule perked up its ears. He kept saying *fine* and then he said *remarkable*—only he said it with a French accent—and pretty soon we were all laughing, Bud loudest of all, but Dale closest to my ear, so I had to push him away a little, since his breath was so awful, and tell him I'd had my dance without him, which caused him to jump up and into the back of the wagon and do a little heel-click and a hop step, then bow and give me a grin. Dale's display induced Bud to try to juggle the whiskey jars and he broke one of them. Having their supply diminished settled them down somewhat and they all sat back on their bench to chew the inside of their cheeks and consider their sins.

"I have not had a drop this whole long night," the speech-maker said as we got started up.

Bud said, "Look here, we can change that real quick."

The neat glugs of the speechmaker and the cheers of the boys beside him was the kind of pleasant prospect I had to consider as we rode along, our company complete, into our final miles. My head had cleared considerably after my dance, and I was holding the map and the boys were happy, and all was good and well and the past with its toothless ladies ran along behind the wagon and couldn't catch up. So when we saw the smudge of white up ahead on the side of the road and Pops, who had taken the reins for a while, slowed the mule down, I got grumpy at the interruption.

"Well, what is it, did someone lose some of their laundry?" I said.

"Quiet down now, Ottie Lee," said Dale.

"It's a Klansman, a real one, looks big, he's on the road to Marvel," Bud said.

"Let's pick him up," said Pops.

If that pointy-head pile of white sheets walking itself along the side of the road heard us come up it did not give any sign of having done so. Its eyeholes looked straight ahead and its arms churned the air alongside it. It must have been wearing dark shoes and socks because you couldn't see them and the whole ensemble looked to be floating just up off the ground. I never could stomach anything wouldn't show its true face to the world, but the boys got excited.

"Climb on up here, friend," Pops said.

No answer.

"We got lots of room," Pops tried again.

"My friends don't lie," said the speechmaker, joining in. He gave a kind of wiggle through the air with his fingers when he said it.

"Stole this rig from a cornflower," said Dale.

"We sure did," said Pops.

Bud gave them each a sharp look. "You were both against it," he said.

"Never mind that now," said Pops. "I was there. You all saw me. I helped do it. And here I am driving this fine rig. What do you say about that, good sir down there, ain't this a fine wagon we got?"

But the sheets didn't look up. Wouldn't. I wondered if he had a bottle under his robes.

"Offer him a sip," said Dale.

"You offer him some of yours," said Pops.

The speechmaker gave a kind of greasy smile at them both and leaned over the side of the wagon and held out the jar he had in his hand. After a minute he gave a shrug and reeled his arm back in.

"Perhaps later," he said.

"Yes, sir, whenever you get the itch."

"Feel that old scratch in your throat."

They had been squawking like that awhile when Bud spoke up.

"Listen, we all up here believe in the great Kluxnation," he said.

The others thought this was putting too fine a point on the pencil, because they kind of looked off to the side when Bud said this, and I just gave out a plain old snort, but that didn't stop Bud, now that he'd got started, from waxing big about the wonders of the Klavern and about all the fine Kluxmen he knew. He said he had met a surefire Wizard once and maybe even set down to a hog supper with a Cyclops. That particular good old boy had eaten fifteen pork chops and called out for more.

"And I'll tell you what," Bud said, "the serving ladies brought it right over to him. I've never seen a man eat as much and treat the others around him as kind."

A true Christian, this likely Cyclops of the Kluxnation had been. The world needed more like him. And more like this man walking with such good strong strides through the dark. The Klan was as good and American as fresh peach pie and it would make him proud, Bud said—while I just kept on snorting—to have one of its members ride to the lynching in a cornflower-stole wagon with him and his friends.

"That was handsomely put," said the speechmaker.

Bud patted the bench beside him and said, "Come on up."

"Shut your stupid mouth or I'll climb up there and rip it

out of your face and feed it to your friends," said the big Klansman.

And with that he left the road and set off across the field and a few seconds later all we could see of him was the bobbing of his pointy head above the corn.

The boys grew glum after this, and if they had sipped at their drinks before we had met the Klansman, now they slurped them down like someone had set loose the spigots at the soda shop. The mule went just as nicely and the wagon just as gently as before, but after that parley, as the speechmaker might have put it, I couldn't conjure any image of a ship or of days gone by with ladies to curtsy and men to bow. Only image came to mind was my father, of all things, late in his days, picking drunk through some salt- and pepper shakers in one of his dusty sample boxes.

You ain't no captain and this ain't no ship and you ain't a fancy lady and the only mystery to it all is why that speechmaker hasn't lost his hairpiece yet, I said to myself. It was just farmland. Indiana. Middle of an August night. Night full of trees and ropes.

First Bud climbed off the bench and went to set in the back of the wagon, then Dale joined him. We bounced along a while like that, then Pops turned to me without a word and handed me the reins. I took them and he climbed into the back of the wagon with the others. The four of them clinked their jars together and set to slurping down all they had left.

"We're about at Marvel," I called back over my shoulder and gave a whack into the dark with the map, but none of them made a sound except Dale, his fine line of jaw lost in the shadows, who let out a long, soft belch. Bud seemed the worst off. He was slumped in the corner of the wagon with his legs splayed out in front of him, not crying again but more like he had got one of his big fists finally pointed at the right target and knocked himself out. I started, even then, to get up a joke about this, but changed my mind and thought I'd do better to let it go. Everyone knew that even though the Klan wasn't much more than a shadow of what it had been, Bud wanted into it and the Klan wouldn't let him in. After he lost his family he had stepped out casual some years before with the sister of one of the big boys in the local Klavern and she had told her brother and that had been that. You crossed the Klan and the Klan closed its doors and you were considered ahead of the game if they just kicked in your teeth and skinned you alive. Bud thought he'd got off lucky with a burning cross in his front yard. But then the next night some boys in masks showed up before the garage cinders had stopped smoldering and tied Bud to an engine block. They each one of them, did those boys, carried a knife, which they brandished before him awhile then put to work. Bud said they didn't do any real damage, just tickled him some, but this was coming from a man put bonus money in my paycheck to drive down the road with him once a month and let him tug on my hair.

Anyone who wasn't a Klansman or—come to think of

it—that boy on his bicycle had told Bud Lancer to shut up, that person would have been sleeping it off until next Sunday. But there Bud lay like he was ready to be stuck with any number of sharp Ticonderogas, and maybe do the sticking himself. Next time I looked over my shoulder, all four of them, even the speechmaker in his fine linen suit, had splayed themselves out like that. They had their heads propped up against the wagon sides and looked like it was all they could do to keep inhaling air and get the jars up to their lips. I dropped the reins into my lap and unrolled the map, thought maybe it could still help me study my way forward, if I could just figure how to read it, but without Dale lighting matches there wasn't much beside the sheen of the pictures around the edges I could make out. Everything in its middle where we were was dark. Even Marvel, where the shimmery lines came together, was obscure, the picture of the courthouse easy to imagine, impossible to see.

Woe to the man with a wobble in his legs." My father liked to say that. In fact, it might have been about the last thing he said out loud on this earth. That night, it could have been Dale's song. Since about a mile on down the road after I thought they were settled, he got roused up enough to half stand, say, "Lordy me," and fall right out of the wagon. He landed with a pillow-punch sound in the ditch grass and I set the brake and climbed off to see whether he had broke his neck. The others in the back hadn't moved a smidge. Bud was sleeping like a baby, Pops looked like his trick in the tree had caught up with him and he was about ready for the embalmers, and the speechmaker was drooling onto his hand and had a long fat leg dangling over the wagon side. Dale was lying still on his face so I put some elbow grease into it and flipped him over. He had a scrape on his cheek and some leaves in his hair. He was looking at me and grinning.

"Some night, wasn't it," he said.

"The night ain't over," I whispered back.

"What's left to do?"

"What's left?"

"That's what I said."

131

He kept grinning. There was bubbles of his whiskey breath popping on my cheeks and nose. There was whiskers of what could have been steam coming out his nostril holes. Some of that steam hit my face and I felt a heat rising up in me.

"Everything," I said and whacked him across the face with the rolled-up map.

The grin came off his face.

"You were rude to that Klansman, Ottie Lee."

"You know I can't stand a Klansman. Last I knew about it you couldn't either."

"Tonight's different. This is Marvel night. Anyway, you know how Bud feels."

"To hell with crybaby Bud Lancer," I said. I hit him with the map again. Hard this time and right on his nose. He grabbed my wrist. I tugged away. The heat hadn't stopped. It had grown stronger. I felt it in my arms. Felt it in my legs.

"You mean that?" Dale said.

"'Course I do."

"So what are you going to do about it?"

"Quit my job."

"You going to quit?"

"I'll quit tomorrow."

"You better quit."

"I *plan* to."

"You think I don't know?"

"Know what? That Bud's the king of the jackasses?"

I hit him again with the map, hard as I could, and this time Dale started laughing like I'd told my best joke.

He stopped laughing when I unbuttoned his pants.

"What are you doing, Ottie Lee?" he said.

"You're an idiot and don't know everything, Dale Henshaw," I said and pulled up my dress. His personal appliance was drooping some, but it wasn't everything about Dale that was small and I'm being honest when I say some droop down there on that hot, dry night was an advantage. I got this picture as I started of Pops and Bud and the fat speechmaker risen from their slumbers and looking over the wagon boards at me in the moon-dark and it made me whack at Dale's face again and ride faster. "There's things you don't know," I said to him. Saying it out loud made me bite on a corner of my lip. "There's lots you don't know," I said. Saying it made my eyes turn right, then left, then right again. It made me grunt and growl and groan.

"She didn't just try to kill me."

"Easy now, Ottie Lee, you got a lot of drink in you," Dale said.

"Easy now to hell with you," I said back. "Let's see what you got now. Let's see you do this. Come on."

Dale was looking up at me, his eyes squinting hard.

"You sure, Ottie Lee?" he whispered.

"Call me Pearl," I whispered back.

That's when someone started shooting at us.

It all went quick then. Like an old movie machine got cranked too fast. "Jesus fuck!" said Dale as a bullet winged up over our heads. He'd been flat as a piece of burned pancake the minute before, but now he flew straight up off the ground like I wasn't on top of him. The gun went off again and Dale jumped back so hard it threw me against the wagon and I cracked my head. It was a big gun with a big report and it didn't need to go off more than that second time for me to leave off rubbing the side of my head and scramble up on the wagon. The mule was going berserk in its yoke and when I dropped the map and pulled off the brake it leaped forward with a lurch that just about launched me into the atmosphere.

The gun went *blam!* again and we flew straight down the road and then off it into the shallow ditch where Dale and I had been lying and up into a bean field. *Blam!* went the gun, and Dale, who had been running behind with his pants unbuttoned, yelped, caught up with us, and climbed aboard. The four boys lay flat in the back of the wagon, hands covering their heads. The gun went off one more time and I felt the night air move next to my ear and thought I heard someone behind us yell out something I didn't understand, a name I couldn't catch, then I must have fainted from that bullet I'd almost caught because next thing I knew, I was waking up in a patch of dirt and bean stalk.

"Goddamn, Dale, I fell out of the wagon too," I said. But no one was there to hear me. The wagon was gone. I stood up and saw where its tracks led off into the dark.

"Hey!" I yelled, but a crop field swallows sound, so it came out quieter than I liked. I yelled again. "Hey, you tin-can fuckers, get back here!" I started to yell once more then remembered that as fast as that mule had been running, we hadn't rolled all that far from where the shooter had been.

"Shit fuck," I said, crouching low. The beans were getting tall but they were beat down by the heat and it came to me I'd have to lie down if I really wanted to hide myself. My dress was already a ruin and I'd lain myself down next to the speechmaker in the road and on top of Dale in the ditch so I didn't see how there was any way some more laying down could hurt. I stretched out on my stomach between the rows and put my cheek down on my hands.

The night had been all noise with never an end to it and now it was nothing but quiet. Just the gentle whooshing of the earth, the tiny stirrings of the beans. I felt cold, then I felt hot. My head hurt and itched at the same time. I'd hit a soft patch when I fell out of the wagon but I knew come morning I'd have about fifteen bruises. For all I knew, those clunkerheads were still lying flat in the back of the wagon with their eyes closed. Probably all saying their prayers. Thinking about them praying made me wonder if I ought to be. Dale and I didn't get over to church much but we went sometimes. I knew my Our Father about as well as the next person. I'd learned it at the Spitzers'. I'd said it at night in my bed hoping my father would come back for me. I'd said it each time my father had left me there alone again. I'd said it plenty frequent after he came to collect me that last time too. "Our Father," I said. Only when I said it, my throat caught and it came out wrong. That annoyed me and I was glad I was alone. Then I wasn't glad. I'd looked earlier out of Sally Gunner's eyes and seen lights in the trees. Where were those lights now? Had those really been bullets before? Or had it been those lights? Firing blasts from heaven. Salvos from the sky. Was that my message? Was that what the Abraham Lincoln angel had meant? I'd frowned and made faces inside a church where others had their heads bowed. I shouldn't have ever let Bud drive me down the lane even if it was just to get groped. No matter how bad we needed the money. I shouldn't have danced with the speechmaker. I should have spoken to my mother. Run down that road after her and Dale. Told her to go to hell. Helped her get there. Told Dale every part of what she had done. There wasn't any way I could quit my job. Not unless Dale sold that pig of his. He ought to sell his pig. Or we ought to eat her. Chop her and roast her right up.

"Our Father," I said again and hell if my voice didn't catch a second time. *I'm dead,* I thought. *I'm lying here dead in my grave and will never rise again. The map is gone with the wagon and I got shot and didn't know it and now I'm as dead as those boys in their tree. Maybe I'm hanging next to them. Maybe some-one sniffed me out. Spoiled goods. Got their gasoline at the ready to douse me. Set me to burn.* Surprise! Maybe *I* was my bright message. Only I wasn't dead. I could hear my heart. My tongue was dry and my ear was ringing.

"Our goddamn Father," I said. This came out fine and I pushed myself up onto my knees and into a crouch again. Scanned the surround. Who knew how far away they might be by now? I was turned around some but the wagon tracks looked to lead off in the direction of Elwood. They'd had plenty of time to come to their senses. To come and fetch me. I'd have gone back for them. 'Course I would have. Still, maybe Dale had understood what I meant and told them, *My wife is the issue of a madwoman. She's afraid she'd do things you don't do. Hurt her own children. Her real name ain't even Ottie Lee.*

Where does it ever end? I was nineteen miles from nowhere; the farce had gone on long enough, it was time to find my way out of the field. Marvel or no Marvel, it was time to go home. I stood up and brushed off my dress and by and by like a bloom birthed out of the long night's dream a young cornflower woman walked by. I didn't see it at first but she was holding a pistol in her hand. When she got up on me she raised the pistol and pointed it in my direction. She held it on me as she kept walking and I didn't breathe, then she pulled the trigger and it went *click* and she smiled and pulled it again then lowered it and stopped smiling and spit and then van-ished down the wagon tracks into the dark.

Home was where I was heading and home was where I would have gone. I believe that. My pillow was calling me. I wanted a bath. I wanted my side of the bed. I wanted Dale lying there next to me, no matter what he had told anyone else, already deep into his snores. Dale and our property would be my Marvel. A smiling cornflower with her gun could be my Marvel. Old ladies and magic pickles. Catfish suppers. Sweet mules and sleeping pigs and slaughter time. My mother gone up to Gary. Dancing on the gravel in the dark. I quickened my step. Shivering despite the heat, so I rubbed my arms. I'd stop shivering. I knew shortcuts. I'd be home before I knew it. I'd have been home.

But just a hundred yards into my retreat I heard a motor. I saw headlights and put out my hand. Of all the souls it could have been, it was Candy Perkins. She had been to Marvel, seen it all, borrowed a car, and left out to get herself freshened up for more fun. Now she was on her way back.

"You look like shit, Ottie Lee, hop in," she said.

I pulled open the door. Climbed in with what I thought was some jaunt to my step. Raised up one of my eyebrows and gave her a saucy smile. Called up one of the remarks I'd meant to make to her when I saw her again. It was about old boy-friends and beauty pageants. But before I had gotten it even halfway out, I had my cheek on her shoulder and was blubbering like Bud. I cried and sobbed so long and loud, she shut off the engine.

"My good Lord, what's got into you?" she asked me.

For a while, though, even after she'd started the car back up and got us going toward Marvel, all I could do was shake my head.

CALLA

I stepped up slow from the river, like it was me not the good green water that had decided to follow its lazy ways. Slow through the day and the day's fierce hell of heat with my feet muddy and my ankles dripping and my forehead on fire from sitting there so long. Fool out there in the beat-down grass. Waiting. There was a horsefly liked the look of my right shoulder and two deerflies trying to sleep in my hair, get all cozied up in my curls, set up in the hot dark, the sweet dark, the devil dark in there. I killed them each one quick, then felt lonely, then laughed a little without any smile to it at myself.

Some old leg-cripple lady I had never seen before was sitting on the porch of a blue house I didn't know, and when I straightened up from my laugh she gave me a good long frown. I stopped a minute and gave her a smile and slow wave to let her know that it wasn't entirely all the cheese had slid off my cracker but also so I could look around and try to see how it was there could be a house I didn't recognize on a road I had walked down many was the time.

"You all right?" said the old woman with her twisted leg. She raised her cane at me when she said it and when she raised her cane up and up into the air over her head I knew it was just the day doing this to me, just the day making its re-arrangements against what it had already offered and what it still had in store.

"Yes, I am all right, and I thank you for asking," I said.

"None of us is all right today, you ask me," she said. "This is a devil day and what have you been doing down there at the river anyway and I'm here visiting my daughter and this shit hell happens and we all ought to leave on out of this town."

"I was having a picnic," I said and held up the basket I had just about forgotten I was holding. Some of the red frill poking out from its lid had river mud on it and the handle had pulled a little loose.

"A picnic!" she said.

"But it was too hot. We gave it up."

"Too hot I'd goddamn guess. What do you mean, you were having a picnic? Day like today. You know what they're getting up to over at the courthouse. They're fetching up their pitchforks. Putting on their horns. A picnic! I've never heard the like. I bet ten goddamn dollars you could fry an egg still snug in its shell on the top of your hat. How hot is it? I know we beat a hundred. And that's just where I'm setting in this porch shade."

"It was cooler down by the river," I said.

"Cooler my country ass," she said. She cackled. She stamped her cane on the porch.

"I put my feet in the mud. It was cool down in there."

"Girl, you need to come out of the heat. Where are your people? You ought to get on back to them and put your head in some shade. We keep it cooler out in the country. You all don't have any breezes. They make you pay for them over in here? Is that why no one here has any? This is a motherfucker of a day. No wonder they're getting their ropes out."

The old lady kept on talking and I smiled and gave her another wave and wished her a nice visit with her daughter and mercy from the skies for all of us, especially the boys they were set to murder, and she lifted up her cane at me and I walked on, up from the river—an easy mile of streets and houses even if it was hell-poker hot and I didn't see anyone else past a dead pigeon and a pair of squirrels flicking tails at each other—and back home.

My idea had been I would hose off, then come in quiet through the back door and get my picnic things put away and the dirty basket hidden and myself cleaned up and then who knew what next, who could know, but the house was empty, there wasn't a one of them there, they were all gone. I'd got a picture in my head when I'd come up from the banks that when I got through the gate I'd walk smack-dab into Aunt V and Uncle D fussing themselves back and forth across the yard, getting ready to leave town, Aunt V fussing small and fast, Uncle D fussing big and slow. Hortensia would be sitting somewhere in the shade while they fussed. Fan in her hand.

Maybe singing. Is how I'd seen it. But there wasn't anyone shade-sitting or singing or fussing in the yard except the old blue jay Uncle D kept wanting to shoot.

"Uncle D?" I called out. "Aunt V? Hortensia? Where are you all?"

I searched the house. Top to bottom. Just like I thought maybe they were playing hide-and-seek on me, were up in the attic behind Uncle D's old war trunks, or in the big second-floor closet behind Aunt V's Sunday gowns, or down in the basement where it was darker and cooler, where the rats took their naps and ate their snacks, where the spiders set up their webs. I went next door and I knocked. I went across the street and knocked there too. No one answered.

"Hey, now," I said and stood in our front yard, in the sun, mud on my feet, basket in my hand, tapping my elbow against some of Aunt V's begonias. They were bright and pink in the burned-out yard. Everything sun-charred like the sky had left its iron on too long. But not those begonias. I felt down into their dirt. She had just watered them. She never watered in the middle of the day. With the wet dirt on my fingers, I went back inside, into the living room, looked up at the light fixture, and there it was. Uncle D had a big glass eyeball with a hook on its top he'd hang when everyone left the house. "To keep watch." Whatever there was to see, it would see it then whisper it all later into his ear.

"Aunt V?" I said. The big glass eyeball spun slowly. They

had really done it. I rubbed hard at my own eyes with the fingers I'd had in the begonia dirt and made a crumbled smear across my face. I went to the kitchen sink and spit then, a good big gob, because I didn't like the taste of sweat mixed with dirt.

W e're going to leave you here," Aunt V had said and I had laughed out loud and Uncle D had said, "No one is leaving anyone," and Hortensia had said, "I'm scared."

"Scared of what?" I had said and Aunt V had said, "That's just like you to ask a fool question," and Uncle D had said, "That *is* a dumb question but she isn't a fool."

"It's not like they're going to lynch us all," I said and Hortensia said, "How do you know that, Calla Destry?" and Aunt V said, "You don't know what they are going to do and that's just the truth," and Uncle D said, "I would like to see them try," and I said, "I'll only be gone an hour."

"For a picnic!" Aunt V said.

"I made a promise," I said.

"What we need to do is go down there and bust them out," Uncle D said.

"I don't want to go down there," Hortensia said.

"I like Uncle D's idea," I said.

"No one is going down there. They got half the cornsilk town and half the cornsilk countryside down at the court-house," Aunt V said.

"Just half?" I said. "We can handle half!"

"We'll give you your hour, then we'll go bust them out," Uncle D said.

"No one is busting anyone out," Aunt V said.

"I'm so scared," Hortensia said.

"One hour," Uncle D said.

I had been gone for two. Maybe more, if I was honest. Sitting down there by the river with my basket. Watching the dragonflies. Counting the reeds. Thinking on the speech I was going to make. What I would say if he said one thing or what I would do if he said another. Sitting there making up songs I didn't have the voice to sing. Waiting for someone who didn't come. Just like the fool Uncle D had said I wasn't.

I'm not a fool, I thought. A car went by. I left the eyeball and the begonias behind and ran to the front gate and looked out after it. It was a cherry-red roadster. Cornflowers I didn't know in the front seat. Nice little car. Couldn't help but think of those boys they were getting their ropes ready for. Those boys had had a speedy car too. I'd seen the older ones plenty around town. Who hadn't? I watched until the roadster got gobbled not too far down the street by a heat mirage.

You know why he didn't come, I thought.

There was still begonia dirt on my face. Warm and wet and done being crumbly now. The front yard had been quiet after the car had passed but suddenly here came the blue jay ugly-winging his way around from the back and set in to screeching like it was him had made his decision and was bragging it up to the neighborhood. The jay was loud and the begonias were bright and I said, "Say we go find him," so I lifted the lid of the basket to make sure the gun was still there. It was sitting snug and dull-shiny in the middle of the two untouched ham-meat sandwiches I had made, each flanked in its turn by my good shoes, which I had put in there for safekeeping.

Set now and feeling firm to my purpose I went inside and got my ankles and feet cleaned up and changed dresses and repinned my hat and changed out my good shoes for my sturdy ones and put them on and went with the basket to the shed in back of the house. The old flatbed usually sat in front of it was gone. Aunt V wouldn't drive, Hortensia couldn't, and Uncle D had bad eyes from the war. So now I knew and no question to it they really had decided to leave. I could see Uncle D hunched up over the steering wheel, hear Aunt V calling out the obstacles. Sometimes he said his glass eyeball saw better than he did. Wasn't for nothing I was the one did all our driving. It was a joke I didn't think too much of in their house that they'd taken me in because I'd been taught how to drive. Aunt V told the joke kind of hard and Uncle D kind of soft but either way I didn't like it. Upshot anyway was they were gone with the truck. Unless I wanted to walk some more and probably die this time in the heat, I was going to have to requisition the Dictator.

The shed wasn't much like the whole neighborhood wasn't much, but it was painted neat brown and had a green tile roof that looked fair pretty in the autumn time when it got itself feathered up all orange with hickory leaves. The shed had a window on each side that had been blacked over and there was a last year's wasp nest under its house-side eave with the back half of a dead citizen still clinging on. I tugged open the big double doors, thought a second maybe I'd find them all in there waiting for me and ready to holler out, "Surprise!" But it was just cobwebs and oil cans and Uncle D's tools and some of Aunt V's hatboxes and a stack of magazines and the smell of stale heat and, in the light pouring over my shoulders and onto the Dictator, whole swirling galaxies of seed tufts and paint flecks and skin chips and powdery orange rust.

The Dictator had never been out in daylight since Uncle D had won the bidding for her at an estate-shutdown auction in Indianapolis. He paid cash on the barrel and we drove it away on out of there and brought it home. *We* here is me. I've already said that. I asked Aunt V once after we were back if she wanted to take a turn at the wheel and that's when she coughed out for the first time, "You're the driver, Calla Destry. That's what we took you in for!"

The Dictator sat there always waiting for us under a soft cloth in the dim, dead air of the shed. It was canary yellow where it wasn't brown leather or chrome. Canary slick yellow everywhere, even its roof. We all of us went along when it was Dictator-driving time. We drove after dark and deep into the night up and down the dark roads with the stars and moon streaming their light in everywhere because everyone knew what stood a hell of a good chance of happening to those sweet wheels if the cornsilks found out about it. Found out we had it living there in the shed. *At our disposal* is the phrase. Aunt V's cousin Merle had bought a nice car and found it two weeks later burned to a devil's dessert in the bottom of a gravel pit. Everyone else we knew had nice cars drove nervous. Looked over their shoulders. Kept their feet close to the gas. Now I was going to drive the Dictator out into the daylight. Which I won't say even then and there with sweat on my face and a gun in my basket didn't make me smile. You can smile anytime. I had smiled down there at the river as I had waited. Waited for my Leander. Many was the time I had said at the supper table that we ought to drive out into the daylight. Drive proud. Proud and *goddamn,* I had said one time, wouldn't it be nice for once to see long into the world we were driving through.

"Watch that language of yours, Calla Destry, you're not in

the orphan house anymore," Aunt V had said. And I had said straight back to her that I would fight anyone who tried to take a torch to the Dictator. I had learned to do plenty besides swear and drive in the orphan house.

Pull off that cloth, let me look at my big yellow baby! said Uncle D.

I gave a jump because I thought Uncle D had come back to me and said this, but when I turned, it was just the lane that led down to the alley that fed out into the street and the houses and the yards and the lanes and buildings of Marvel. I pulled off the cloth. I already had the keys in my hand. As I stepped up close to Uncle D's yellow baby that he wasn't there to admire—and so to hell with him—I could see from my reflection in the window glass that I should have done a little more tugging at my hair before I repinned my hat. The heat had had its way. It had gotten flatter than I felt good about. The Dictator's soft leather seats gave a creak as I climbed in.

The street was empty. Nobody out but old Turner Jenkins trickling false hope onto his doomed geraniums with a beat-up watering can. I kept my eyes good and peeled as I rolled past the heat-burned yards and quiet wooden houses on the way to the courthouse. I had told Uncle D as soon as we heard what was coming that morning that I wanted to see what it looked like and he had told me it wouldn't be anything but ugly and Aunt V had said, "You don't need to go looking for a lynching mob in this country. Lynching mob always finds its way to your doorstep or down the street. Anyway, you got your picnic to get to!"

"I made a promise," I said back to her.

"A promise!" She snorted.

"I said I would be there!"

"The things you say!"

"You say you're going to do something you have to do it."

"That's true, that is," Uncle D said.

I repeated what he had said out loud. It was good into the afternoon but the sun felt like it wasn't much more along than the middle of the sky. Like it had down by the river. Like the angels had left the fiery door to heaven open up there in the blue beyond.

Leander liked to talk about the sun and its doings. He had a theory for every minute of the night and day. He had about half the whole world in his head and he would blow gusts of it out into my ear when we took a walk. He would say, "Stop, now, listen, do you hear that? You think that's the wind in the maples, but it's not the wind. It's the universe twitching."

Which is what the universe was doing down at the courthouse square, and before I knew much more than half of what was happening, I turned onto Lincoln and got snarled up in the middle of it. Why that turn? I don't know. No Leander, but cornsilks by the hundreds and more cornsilks stepping their way in. Like they had decided to hold the county fair at the courthouse but kill people instead of showing cows and pigs. None of it was what I had expected. None of it was what I had thought, which was Klan hats and Klan robes and Klan torches and maybe a few ugly cornsilk men with bleeding, chaw-filled mouths. No, this was cornsilks drinking out of bottles in the bright sunshine. Cornsilk families reclining in the shade of the killing trees. There were women and babies and little boys juggling apples and bulldogs slobbering and biting at their own tails. This wasn't something away on *over there,* like a picture show—this was all around, this was right next to me.

I drove slow because that's all I could do and went past a little girl in a green dress who was draped like limp lettuce over her father's shoulder. She gave me a sleepy smile, lifted her little hand, and said, "Hi," in a soft voice as I went by and I rolled up my window. There was a mailman standing next to her father holding a picture of the governor, and a tall gal in a fancy blue dress next to him. I saw people I recognized everywhere I looked: a man from the hardware store where Uncle D bought supplies; a teenage girl who sold papers at the interurban station; a boy who was always on his bright orange bicycle and who was on it today.

"This is about to get ugly," I said. And about when I said it somewhere deep in the crowd someone started to yell about something and I looked over behind me and there was a woman standing on the hood of a parked black Ford and she was dancing and spinning around and beating at the air with her arms. She danced with her mouth open and her eyes raised heavenward like she had a direct line to the lord of lynchings and whippings and beatings and burnings and then she toppled over and fell and pretty soon after she fell, the yelling she'd got started stopped.

But I kept hearing it in my head. Keep hearing it. Down the years and always banging at my door. And when it comes, when I'm thinking back, the devil-hot, blister-bright after-noon sky I am driving through turns to black and the air grows scorching ever hotter and the cornsilks' heads glow red with the heat of it and they cackle and roar and move in their glowing thousands for the jail. The earth starts to shake when they go. The Dictator commences to rise up into the air and slam down. Up and slam down and I can barely get the door open but I leave the Dictator and go with them. I am in the crowd and above it and the sheriff steps aside and they take their sledgehammers to the walls and beat their way in. Then they are pouring across the tile floors and past the iron doors and through the hallways of the big jail and there I go pour-ing with them and as we pour there are shouts about God and about country and about honor and about truth and about death and death and death and we pour up the stairs and find where they are holding the boys. I'm not dreaming, it's something I'm seeing, I'm there and I tell them to stop and I'm not alone in telling them. There are hundreds of us, thou-sands, many thousands, millions even, and the earth joins us and the sky and the moon and the stars and we say stop but they do not stop. The first boy is beat to death right there, then dragged around, then hung from the bars on the cell window. Then one by one they take the others. They drag them dead and about-to-be dead through the night and the heat and the roaring crowd and the universe twitching to the killing trees.

If it's yelling brings it all to black, it's a scream restores that day to its earlier sunlit evil self. It came out of the mouth of an old lady. I hear it in my head and the sun rips straight through the black overlay. She was a soft-looking thing and round and bent over plenty and on the short side to start with but she had a tornado in her throat. She screamed and this time instead of still rolling, I stopped the Dictator sharp. She had her hand up in the air and was pointing at the jail. So I turned and looked that way this time and a bloody shirt now hung long and limp from a top-floor window. An ensign of what hadn't yet happened but was about to. It looked from where I was like a cut of pork or a side of beef. The old lady screamed again and a younger woman yelled out that it was the killed cornsilk boy's shirt, the one he had been wearing when the cornflowers had shot him and then had their fun on the ground with his girl. That bloody shirt snapped those cornsilks out of whatever spell had been keeping them from looking my way. Like a fresh and hard wind was blowing through them, they all turned their heads from the jail toward me.

"That's a goddamn cornflower in that car," said someone right close.

"Got to go." I said this well and loud to myself but it took me longer than I liked to see it happen. My arms had turned to stone or got gooped up in a dream. It had dropped quiet outside the car after that "goddamn cornflower." But it was a rumbling quiet, quiet had lightning for a tail. Boy named Roscoe I had started running with when I still lived at the orphan house was like that. He would get real quiet, like it was a well to China had opened up in front of him, and he would smile slow down into that well and then look up fast and hit whoever or whatever was closest to him if whoever or whatever was closest to him was too stupid to get out of his way.

Some of the cornsilks in the crowd were smiling. Just the way Roscoe smiled when he was making a fist. I couldn't get myself to drive but I did get a hand off the steering wheel and started for the basket. If they wanted lightning they could add some of mine to their storm. And gooped up or not, I would have fuck sure helped them make it, that lightning, if that little girl I had seen on her father's shoulder a minute before hadn't stepped out just then from between some long legs. I saw her and I swallowed hard and took my hand away from the basket and put it back on the Dictator's wheel. Because she still looked sweet, this little girl, sleepy too. I sometimes babysat for cornsilk folk that Aunt V worked for cleaning houses and stores around town, as bad matched for the job as I was, and I had held more than one sleepy cornsilk child just like her after a nap. As I watched, though, that

159

pretty little girl spit on the ground and scrunched up her face. Then she reared back and I saw she was holding a rock.

She threw hard for such a young thing. Her rock hit the Dictator on the driver's-side door. There was some fat silence after the rock hit, then shouts of approval popcorned up from the oil and you could tell quick by the number of heads scanning the ground that those good folks were about to start raining rocks on me.

"Drive away now, Calla," I said. There was a calm in my voice this time and command too. I put the car in gear and opened up the throttle. Few ugly cornsilk boys kicked the front fender, and the Dictator got hit by a hot dog and whacked with a stick as I tire-spun it away, but no more rocks, they hadn't gotten their hands on them in time. On the subject of hands, mine started to shake as soon as I was clear of the crowd and away from the square. I saw a picture show once where a woman slapped a man had got the shakes and I wished someone would slap me but there wasn't any someone there. Shaking, I let my free hand kind of butterfly-flap itself away from the wheel over to the glove box. Uncle D kept his silver war flask in there. He kept it full of good, sharp whiskey and liked to take a drink while we drove. Said it helped him warm his throat and cool his head and collect his thoughts. It didn't do any of those things for me but I drank anyway and coughed hard when I caught some of the burn. Water started coming out of my eyes and I wiped at it with the back of my hand and then drank and coughed again, then said, "Now get yourself the fuck on away from here."

Instead, after I had driven fast away a few blocks and was shut of all but a few cornsilk stragglers heading toward the show, I took one more drink, put the flask down, and pulled over in front of a little red house just about swallowed up in ivy. I turned off the Dictator, then I shut my eyes and counted out loud into the empty car until I felt my eyes stop watering and my hands stop shaking. When they had stopped I lifted the flask back up and took another sip, swallowed different, poured it slow down the trough of my tongue this time. Slipping over my tongue and down my throat, it didn't burn as much.

I didn't give the little girl's ugly dent in the yellow door more than a glance as I opened one of the basket flaps just to be ready and, sixteen-year-old fool that I was, went walking back the way I had just come. There must have been something new going on down by the jail besides the bloody shirt flag because there was some shouts and cheers but I didn't pay them any mind. I get an idea in my head, I get focused. I stand tall and walk straight. Always been like that. I walked straight down the street back toward the square with my head down and my chin set and ready to reach into my open basket if anyone stepped in my way. I went across the backside of the square, where there wasn't hardly anybody milling and no blankets spread and no dogs or juggling or ice cream or nasty little girls, and down some steps, under a heat-shriveled grape arbor, and into the courthouse through the east-side door. Any other afternoon, the courthouse would have been full and maybe a fat guard to get past on top of it, but this wasn't any afternoon, and as I climbed up the back stairs with my basket, up and up, I saw not a soul, only a mop and its bucket on one of the landings near the top floor.

I had been to the courthouse many a time that past year with Uncle D, who lettered office glass and did touch-up painting of all kinds after closing. I could have peeked out onto any floor I climbed past and seen his handiwork. It was all over the building. All over town. He could see better than fine right up in front of him and had let me and Hortensia too make some brushstrokes over his shoulders, but mostly we had haunted the courthouse nooks and crannies, hollered in its attics, whispered loud in its corridors and basements and stairwells. It was like being inside the brain of the county and we were its thoughts. Or its dreams. Maybe its nightmares. Meaning, anyway, I knew where I was going: up and up to a big storage room on the north side that Hortensia and I called the flag room because there wasn't anything else in there but flags.

State flags. They were all on sturdy floor stands leaning this way and that. Had spearheads on their tops. Like a forest and field of bright flowers both and many was the time we had played a game of walking quiet through the heavy cloth and pole trunks with our eyes closed. It could take a while to find each other in the big room. Even if you cheated and cracked your eyes open a little, which we both sometimes did. Sometimes we would stop a minute and say what colors we saw or what things. There were blues and yellows and whites and greens and reds. There were animals and buildings and torches and crosses and spires. There were stars everywhere on those flags. Hortensia's favorite was from the state of New Mexico. It was bright, bright yellow with just a knobbed circle on it, piece of fire painted red. Mine was the one from South Carolina. Darkest blue and just had on it a palmy white tree and a sharp-curved white moon. All you need. One tree and the moon.

Sometimes when Hortensia had stayed down with Uncle D or was wandering off elsewhere I'd go and sit by it. Or wave it back and forth, pull it out away from its stand. Tried to imagine what it might be like to step into it, get myself down to South Carolina, sit quiet under a palm tree in the night. It came up close, when I stretched it, to the Indiana flag. They were both blue but the Indiana flag was lighter-colored and had a torch looked hot to the touch on it and some more of those stars. Like it was all about what you would do if you

163

strayed in the night. South Carolina was about sitting quiet and not closing your eyes but still dreaming, and Indiana was about being lost. Uncle D had come up with us one time and said they weren't either one about what I'd said and I didn't want to go down to South Carolina anyhow under any circumstances and not to mess with them — they had been for a display and might be used again. As soon as he'd left I went back into the middle of the forest. If I leaned the South Carolina stand a little I could make it and Indiana touch.

I got up there that afternoon and the flag forest was looking some the worse for wear since I'd last seen it. California with its yellow bear was on the floor. So was the big red star of Texas and the yellow eagle of Oregon. Alabama was twisted up and leaning against a wall. It looked like a football team had run through the room. I walked the forest sideways, trying not to touch anything, then went to the window, gave it a good push, couldn't budge it, tried again, got it open, and leaned my head out.

The crowd was like ants on spilled sugar. The treetops above them were dull and green. The roofs stretched out brown and gray and black and there was the smokestack from Fuller's off in the distance made the whole municipality look, if you tilted your head, like it had a burning cigar stuck in its mouth. There was some honking and I saw someone else had had the bad idea to try and drive through the crowd, but it must have been a cornsilk because all the ants did was wave their antennas and step out of the way as the rectangle of the car roof came forward. At the orphan house we poured cups of water on swarming ants whenever we could. We asked them if they had their ark ready. I thought then of pouring water down from above. Onto those ants had lynching on their little minds. As I leaned out the window, one of them, might have been the father of the little girl had dented Uncle D's Dictator, reared skyward on its back legs and waved up at me.

My idea—if you can call it that when you are sixteen and storm-bent on something you haven't thought halfway through—in making that climb had been a small one, maybe throw something out the window and see what it hit, but it grew bigger as I cast my eyes down. Saw how many of them there were. Every last one of them ready to break down the jailhouse door. Do a dance under that bloody shirt, get quick as they could to the killing to come. I'd give them something else they could do their devil-dancing to. It didn't take a minute to retrieve the frizzle-head mop I'd seen on the stairs and find some rope. It was harder than I liked getting the great state flag of Indiana off its floor stand, though, and I wished more than once as I yanked and tugged that I had a good pair of scissors or a knife. Still, I did get it off more or less intact and then fixed it tight around the mop handle so that it looked like a robe or dress around a dead creature. Creature

165

of the state-flag forest. I got the rope snug around her neck and hung the whole thing out the window. Then I took a deep breath, called out, banged hard on the window frame, and laughed good and loud and long at what I had done.

The Dictator could fly if you held it open, which is what I wanted to do once I had gotten down out of the courthouse and back safe to it, hold it wide open and get myself a hundred miles out into the countryside, maybe five hundred, a thousand, head for South Carolina, but a funny thing happened when I got the machine going again. Out in the broad daylight and in the heat, and with my hands holding the wheel steady but my heart pounding fierce from the stairs to the street, my focus left me. Worse, some of that rearranging that I'd felt hit me as I came up from the river earlier returned and it wasn't just one house I didn't recognize, it was the streets I'd known all that last year in Marvel didn't seem the same. And this isn't me thinking back on a piece of the past and covering it over with its about-to-be. This was happening right then. The streets came up curved, like I was looking at them through water, or if they were curved already they came up straight. They were most of them empty, hardly a soul to be seen, and I lost my bearings. I passed the signs for streets I felt sure I knew well, only when I got onto them they seemed too wide or too narrow. There was a big gray house on a corner with handsome scalloped wood and a blue roof I knew belonged to a cornsilk lady had been nice to Aunt V and even sent her a card at Christmas, only when I got up on it I saw the wood scallop was rotting and the roof was covered in moss and someone had thrown a kitchen stool up onto it. A ways down the road from this wreck and right in the middle of town was a deep woods I'd never laid eyes on before.

"You need to get yourself a good deep breath, Calla Destry," I said, which is what Aunt V would have had me do and had done fifty times if it was a dozen since I left the orphan house to live with her and Uncle D and take their charity, but what I did instead of her deep-breathing trick was reach again for Uncle D's flask. Draining it, I crossed the river, which seemed darker and wider than ever it had before, and still didn't get any sense of where I was until I saw Fuller's smokestack rising big-ugly out of the ground almost right up on top of me and knew where I was and that I had to double back. Soon as I was over the bridge again, I yanked hard on the steering wheel and took off down a dirt road, then turned again and found myself heading into a dead end. There was a little dog sitting in some Queen Anne's lace where the gravel stopped. It was working a bone or stick or God knows what, I couldn't tell, and when the Dictator came too close it jumped up, barked considerable more than necessary, and took a bite, I expect, at one of its tires.

"All right, now," I said. For as soon as she started barking I knew that little snaggletoothed dog. She belonged to Big Bob Franklin, and Big Bob Franklin was Uncle D's friend. And just like that, everything snapped back into place. I didn't see any woods. That house wasn't rotting. The river wasn't any wider than it ever was. I put the Dictator in reverse and backed it out of that dead end and retraced my road a ways and got myself over to Bob's and parked the car where it couldn't be seen too easy from the road. His bait store hadn't looked like much the last time I had been by it and now it looked worse. Simple, busted, and shabby.

There was a scrub plum tree growing up one side of it and black moss didn't look any too happy to be alive on its roof shingles. A sign over the door read BOB FRANKLIN'S BAIT SHOP, NIGHT CRAWLERS AND SPECIALTIES. The sign was neatly painted but it had been shot a time or two or a woodpecker had gotten after it or both. I could smell the old river curling slow and green nearby. I cleared my throat. I left my basket in the car. The little dog came up friendly now and gave my shoe a sniff. She had short legs and a long nose and blue eyes. I cleared my throat again and gave her a scratch and went across some crispy grass to a door at the side of the house.

Bait shop. I haven't set my foot in a one since practically that day, but I suspect they still have them. Full of bric-a-brac. Old coffee cans stacked to the ceiling and spit jars and dirt spill and that old lunch and a pair of shoes and some boxing gloves and a row of Bob's friendly bottles. Strips of flypaper, clumpy and black, done their job too well and more old lunch and a model boat never got its mast and mainsail. Some seed catalogs and a box of bullets and worm smell and bell jars everywhere for the whiskey everyone knew Bob made on the side and some pretty-lady pictures probably hadn't been looked at in many a season. A royal-size icebox off in the shadows and a stack of county-fair pamphlets and a pile of yardsticks and a faded picture of old president Theodore Roosevelt. There was a big door that still had its handle set on some sawhorses for a desk. It had its own piles of bric-a-brac but most of it was covered up by a kind of a hand-drawn map or picture painting, it looked like, and a bowl full of some-thing wet. By the desk stood a couple rusted outside chairs on the seats of which now sat smashed some old grandmother's once-favorite pillows. I'd just climbed out of the Dictator but I sank straight down into one of these chairs like I had been standing up for a week with a weight on my head. The chair probably hadn't ever been comfortable but I had about got settled and had even shut my eyes a few seconds when the door to the rest of the house swung open and there was Big Bob. He stood in the doorway a minute looking in my direction before he spoke.

"You by yourself, Calla Destry?" he said. The way you say something everyone present knows the answer to. I nodded, sucked in at my cheeks, shrugged. Bob had a drafting pencil behind one of his ears and as he stood there looking at me he fetched it and started in to tapping with it on the doorjamb.

"That makes two of us," he said. He had a high-pitched voice that skittered and warbled around the edges. I nodded again. If there was an aspect that was big about him you couldn't much see it. There could have been a little something strong in his shoulders or some extra yardage to his eyebrows, but for the rest of it he might have been a wrinkle-faced child playing grown-up.

"You all right, girl?" he said.

I started to ask him why he was asking, the way you do, but my voice fell down in my throat like someone had stuck out a leg and tripped it up. I'd had my hands on the arms of the uncomfortable chair but now I gathered them into my lap and looked down.

"I was sleeping," he said. "Trying to sleep away this day, wasn't getting too far on the project. Got somewhere into some sleep but not anywhere near far enough. There's dreams in that kind of sleep but they're as like to smack you in the mouth as tell you you're special, so I try to avoid them. You ever have dreams like that?"

I nodded. He gave the doorjamb another whack with his pencil then put it behind his ear again and came in and leaned over his map picture.

"This bad boy is wearing me out," he said. "It's not the idea, it's the getting it right. I'm going to put pictures of us around its edges. Found them in the illustrated pages. I've got a stack somewhere around here I already cut small. Going to make a frame of our faces."

He gave a show of looking for the stack of pictures, lifting up the edge of the paper and looking under it and pulling at the desk drawer. When he didn't find anything except a little pot of silver paint like the ones Uncle D used in his lettering work, he took a seat at his desk and put his pinkie finger in the bowl.

"Some of my shine in here," he said. "I took a sliver and we'll see if the shine helps her find her way out. You ever try shine for a sliver?" He lifted his wet pinkie out of the whiskey when he said this. It dripped twice and I realized I had been smelling whiskey since I walked in. I hadn't particularly noticed it since it was the same smell I had on my lips. I could see even from my chair that Bob's pinkie was bad swollen. On the world side. That was what Uncle D called any part of you that faced outward. The you side was just yours; the you side looked in. Bob put the pinkie back in the whiskey, then before I had answered his question, he asked me what had brought me to his bait shop by myself. He said he thought it wasn't for the worms and could smell even far away as I was that I had already had some of his shine. I found my voice and told him I had been late coming home and was out now looking for Uncle D and Aunt V and Hortensia. I don't know why I told him I was looking for them. I wasn't. They had left me behind.

"Trouble again?" he said.

I shrugged. Of course there had been trouble. I was nothing but trouble. From one end of me to the other.

"Well, I haven't seen them," he said.

I told him I hadn't thought he would have, that I had just been out riding and looking for them and decided to stop by.

"Out riding?" he said.

"I got lost. Turned around. I think it was the heat."

Bob leaned back in his own chair, lifted his hands, the right one dripping from the pinkie, put his index fingers together, touched them to the angel mark under his nose.

"It wasn't the heat," he said.

"Wasn't it?"

"You know that, don't you? It's important that you know it."

"What was it, then?"

"You've been hot before, I reckon?"

"Yes, sir." And when I said it I thought straightaway of nights at the orphan house at Indianapolis in my room in the attic with Hortensia already set in to kicking at me and there

173

was just the one little window and no water so we wouldn't wet and we weren't allowed to leave our room and how I thought we might die in our beds by morning from the heat.

"We all been hot before. I once spent sixteen hours chained up in Georgia in a tin shed. It's hot out there today, sure, but, honey, it wasn't the heat roiled up your head."

He let his ailing finger ease back down into the whiskey bowl but kept his left hand where it was against his lips. Then he looked at me, long and quiet. So I told him where I had been and what I had seen and what I had done. I told him about the old lady and the blue house and the little girl with her rock and about the flags and even about the mop and the rope. He nodded his head like it was every day the world had lynchings and nasty little girls and flag forests in it, and when he nodded, the pencil behind his ear joggled loose a little and he lifted his hand out of the whiskey and pulled it across his body, pinkie dripping onto the floor as it went, and pushed the pencil back and then put his finger back in the whiskey, never moving the other hand from his angel mark.

"You went down to the courthouse square on a lynching day looking for them?" he said. "Even light-colored as you are, that's crazy."

Bob let the tip of his tongue poke out a minute and lick a little at his upper lip.

"Not for them," I said.

Bob nodded.

"If I was you and had keys to a vehicle and had just hung a

174

mop with the state flag on it out for all to see and maybe had a fresh quarrel with your foster parents and were looking for others you needed to see bad enough to be deep-foolish, I'd leave town and quick, Calla Destry," he said. He shrugged. There wasn't anything *I don't care* about his shrug. It was a shrug said *It's your life and your home troubles and your lynching day and it's up to you.*

"You think they'll lynch them for sure and true?" I said.

"Sure as I'm sitting here in my junk shop," he said. "Sure as the crawlers I got over there in the icebox. Sure as this house and that yard and that river."

He held his finger up out of the whiskey, and wet trickle lines went down his wrist.

"What I'm saying is you're lucky, girl, they didn't catch you and take you and hurt you and then string you up too."

I nodded. Imagine having your arms broke and your head beat and being lifted up by your neck into the air. Or imagine them doing other things to you. They'd burned a boy alive down in Mississippi just the January before. It had been in the paper all the way up here. Aunt V had read the story to us aloud. She had had to stop four times while she read it. They had called him an "arch fiend" and a "cornflower devil." The paper said it was over two thousand cornsilks at the party.

I asked Bob what he was going to do, if he was going to try to go back to sleep, and he didn't answer and I thought maybe he was thinking about getting neck-tied or about the boy down in Jackson, that we were both sitting there in his bait shop seeing ourselves getting burned or hauled up into the sky. Instead he said, "You ever eat an orange, Calla Destry?"

"A what?" It came so fresh out of the bait-shop blue that I thought a second it wasn't true what Uncle D said that Bob never took a drop of his own whiskey. But there wasn't an inch of him looked drunk.

"You never have, have you?"

I shook my head, slow. Bob slapped the desk with his dry hand, made the little pot of silver paint topple over, righted it, stood, went over to the icebox where he kept his worms, dug around in it, pulled something out, then stepped over to me and held it out. I was sixteen years old and had never seen an orange up close before. He put it in my hand and I started to say something but didn't know what it would be so I just looked at it. Felt its strange, skin-snug weight. Ran a finger pad over all its little bumps. Squeezed. Pushed my nail at its flowery navel, there where the skin turns hard, sharp even, rough. I might even have started into trying to open it, but Bob shook his head and took the orange back.

He went over behind his desk and swept off a corner and set it down. There was some light coming in through the window behind me and the orange rolled a little and the light caught some of its curve and set it to burn. While I watched, Bob pulled a paring knife out of a drawer and cut straight through the light. The back of his hand glowed sharp a second then he set the two sides he had made next to each other on the desk, pulled his chair up close to the corner, and sat down.

"I used to eat a fresh orange every day," he said, and after the minute of quiet his warbler voice seemed like it flew out of his mouth and went flitting around the room. It flitted and he worked with his knife on the orange. I couldn't see everything he was doing to it because of a stack of maroon-color ledger books and a busted-handle coffee cup. He worked and talked. I couldn't take my eyes off what I could see of the orange, of the knife, of his graceful movements. It came over me how tired I already was, like the long day was into its evening instead of just its afternoon.

"While back, this was," Bob said. "Deep down south. I did fishing work on the Florida coast. You know where Florida is? I ate many an orange down there on that coast. You could pick them straight off the tree if they weren't falling down into your hand. But it wasn't until I had had one of old Mr. Chan's oranges that I truly acquired the taste. Mr. Chan was a corntassel had a noodle restaurant I frequented."

I looked at him. *Frequented* wasn't a word you heard every five minutes. Roscoe had liked to use words like that. Sometimes I wrote down the words he used at night after I had made it home. I had kept some of that list and shown it to Leander, who said it was a fine list and indicated a fine mind. I told him that Roscoe's occupation had been punching people in the face who didn't fall in line with him around the streets of the city. Leander said that while that was certainly regrettable (which was also one of the words on the list), it didn't change the principle (which was another), as many a fine mind lay behind punishing fists. Leander had then complimented me on my own fine mind, had said he was a great admirer of my "sparkling wits and talents."

"Noodle restaurant?" I said.

"Everything came with noodles. Even the noodles came with noodles. You didn't like noodles, you were out of luck."

"So this Mr. Chan served oranges with his spaghetti?"

"They were the dessert. He brought them out after you were done and had settled up. You didn't settle up, you didn't get one of Chan's oranges. That was the house rule. Tell you what, we all finished up and paid quick."

Big Bob smiled, then leaned back in his chair. He put both his hands out into the air palms down. Then he flipped his right hand back over and drew a good-size circle on it with his left. Through the circle he drew two lines. Then into this crosscut circle he dipped an imaginary fork.

"It was half an orange, set fat-side down, cut into quarters, served chilled and juicy in a bowl made out of its own peel. I never before nor since tasted the like. You want to try?"

I nodded. He gestured with his chin and I leaned forward and found myself looking at what he had just pantomimed. Only thing different from the way he had showed it was on each half, he had put a big darning needle into one of the orange pieces instead of laying down a fork.

"Go on now," he said.

I could smell that orange even before it was in my hand and just the smell was about enough to knock me down then make me jump straight back up. It was like some sweet treacly fire had been floated up my nose. Bob picked up his half and plucked up a piece and put it in his mouth. I did the same. Pushed it through my lips, touched it to my tongue. It was a day of ugly firsts for me in Marvel but that fat wedge of orange flesh was the sweetest first I've ever known. To this day I can't eat on an orange without thinking about that one. Bob got it, my first orange, and a few others, he said, from a fellow owed him money. He told me to always take the orange when it was offered to you. Didn't matter where you were or how much you were owed or what kind of goddamn day it was.

"Amen to that," I said, chewing slow. There might have been boys in the jail and cornsilk killers getting set to come for them and a little-girl dent in the Dictator door and a gun in the basket out on its front seat, and still I picked up those sweet, heavy pieces and still I put them in my mouth. We didn't either one of us smile as we ate but we did study each other, our eyes bright in the dark of the shop.

"You done?" he said when I had been done five minutes at least and was just sitting there looking at the peel bowl in my hand and licking my lips. I told him I was and he said, "You can toss that peel in the can over there," and I said I would just as soon hold on to it a minute, and he nodded. Then he wiped his hands careful on a towel didn't look too clean and when he had finished his wiping he reached over and put his swollen pinkie into the bowl of whiskey and looked down at the big piece of paper.

"If I get done on this or give it up I'll probably head my way over to a spot near Ryansville. Desmond ever take you there? Good spot to fish and wait things out."

"Ryansville?" I said.

"I been working on this map, been working on it since this morning, since I heard, I was probably even working on it when I was trying to take my nap," he said.

"Map?" I said. I could see he had painted *Marvel* in its middle and that it had many a black mark on it but that was about all.

He didn't answer me, just looked down at the big piece of butcher paper in front of him and held his finger in the bowl and told me exactly where the fishing spot was, just in case. Then he asked me if I had seen his dog, Myrtle. I told him I had and he nodded and said she was probably outside working her bone or under the plum tree and then he picked up a pencil wasn't the one behind his ear and made some kind of a mark on the butcher paper and right when he did that I heard a cry. I heard it sure. It came from outside. From the river. Good and deep and green down there where it rolled.

Bob didn't look up from his work as I left, just said maybe he'd see me later. I said maybe he would and went out the door with the orange-peel bowl in my hand. The air was hot and the street was empty. If there had been a breeze, the grass and bushes and trees and sky, for all I knew, would have crackled loud enough when it came past to make me fear for my ears. But there wasn't any breeze. Just the scraping of katydids and the *tap-tap-tap*-ing of some hard-beaked bird didn't know it was too hot to work. I stood up tall and wiped at my mouth where there was some of that sweet orange stick-iness caught. Then I wiped at my eyes. It must have been a hundred yards from where I stood next to Big Bob's to the river. And down there at the river I saw Hortensia's bright blue hat.

It had been her favorite hat when we were at the orphan house and she had kept it all this time. As I looked at it I heard that cry again. It was long and shimmery and came in and out like someone had thrown a piece of floppy metal up into the sky. I went hurrying across the street and down a sloping field and stumbled in my sturdy shoes, practically running even though I had that orange peel pressed tight

181

against my chest. I had been a good runner at the orphan house and even Roscoe couldn't beat me when I was out with him. Still, you couldn't run sprint-speed holding on to a careful-cut orange peel you didn't want to crush, plus even if it wasn't just the heat had been cooking my head, it *was* hotter out than fresh-baked bricks, and it took me a while to get down to the river. Where I didn't find any Hortensia. What I had seen and maybe heard too was a jay in some sprawly-armed spirea. Cousin, no doubt, to the one Uncle D wanted to shoot — especially after he had spent time at Bob's — and it cocked its head at me then hopped up to a higher spot and cocked its head at me again.

"Goddamn bird even if you are pretty," I said. I walked down to the river and plucked a leaf off a Japanese maple and stuck the darning needle through it and stuck the mast I'd made in the orange-peel bowl and set it down in the water then stood up straight again and watched it float.

I'd pondered on paper boats when I was waiting earlier for Leander and on how Hortensia and I had always tried to see how much we could load into one and it still float. Paper could carry a lot. I wasn't so sure about orange peel. The current was slow but true and it took the little cup of orange and carried it away. I watched after it and splashed my hands into the water and ran them over my forearms. I splashed my hands down again then ran them over my neck. Some of the water found its way down my back and gave me a cool chill so I did it again. I watched the boat go and felt cool for about a minute, that's all, because when the boat had disappeared and I turned away from the water and looked back up the slope to Big Bob's I saw a white car pull up and some cornsilks climb out.

It was three of them climbed out of that car and one of them walked straight over to the Dictator like I hadn't tried to hide it, and I realized that whether or not you'd have had legitimate trouble seeing it from the street, they had probably had a prize view from the lane that sloped down the ridge behind Bob's house. The one that had walked over to the Dictator looked like he was saying something, and the others went over and one of these others looked like he punched at about the place the little girl had made her dent and the third one tossed something up onto the hood. Then it looked like they all took turns spitting on it, and then Myrtle started barking and Bob came out of the shop. The cornsilks turned and when they had all turned I set my chin and with my arms free now ran as fast as I could along a curved line of trees that fringed the long, low slope up to Bob's. Myrtle was barking at the cornsilks and Bob had his hands up in the air and even as I was running the curve of the trees I thought about his whiskey-wet swollen finger swimming the airs over his picture map, how lonesome and wise it had seemed. Two of the cornsilks' fingers now jabbed over in the direction of the Dictator or of what they had tossed up onto the hood, and Bob looked like he laughed or I couldn't tell what, and I ran toward them along the side of the trees like a hot wind. They got bigger and bigger, and I saw at least two of them were the boys that had jumped out of the way when I sped up at the courthouse square. Bob nodded to them calm-like and stepped aside and waved those cornsilks one after another into his shop. He waved them in and Myrtle followed too, then Bob stopped and turned and looked straight at me and pointed at the Dictator, then made a gesture like he was dropping his fishing line into the water. Then he went in after the cornsilks.

I didn't stop running, didn't slow a goddamn step, even if my heart did make a flip, up and over and into the air, when I saw what it was they had tossed up onto the Dictator. I grabbed it and kept running around the other side of the car and when I was in I sat a minute on the driver's seat and looked at it, at the mop with its star-covered dress still cinched snug around its neck. I pulled it into the car after me and set it down hard on the passenger side and there it sat, looking out the windshield back toward the river. *That's where I ought to drive us,* I thought. Lot about that day and everything since would have changed if I'd done that. Straight down the slope and into the river and maybe we could've found Hortensia and chased the orange-peel boat, chased it all the way down to the Wabash where our fine green river fed into its end. Picture of that peel boat came into my mind brought me back to Big Bob. I looked away from the river and at my basket. It sat next to the mop. I thought about Bob talking to those boys and looked at my basket and then I like to have screamed at myself because my hand betrayed me and instead of reaching for what was in the basket it went to the ignition.

Uncle D's big old yellow baby jumped up fast. It always started quickly. I was rolling and had myself a good start when those cornsilk boys came pouring back out of Bob's house, each one of them holding a bottle in a paper bag. I saw Bob reach for one of them and get himself punched at for it, and I saw Myrtle bite at one of them and get herself kicked. I started to slow and cursed myself for a fool and a coward and now my traitor hand did go into the basket but it was shaking again like shaking was the only thing it could do, and then the cornsilks were all back in their car anyway and they set it straight to rolling hard, so I looked to the road and not backwards any longer and held the Dictator open, and the Dictator roared.

I drove like I meant it then. The road curved, then ran straight, then curved again, then crossed the river and I went as hard as I knew how the whole time. If the police hadn't been busy raising toasts and handing out sledgehammers down at the jail I probably would have had myself more than just those boys in their white car to see me out of town. It hadn't looked like much of a vehicle they were driving but they must have stuffed in some extra horses under its hood because as fast as I went, they stayed always a few hundred yards behind me. You might have thought with my shaking hands and cowardly ways and that mop doll setting alongside me I would have got lost again, but even if I was huffing and sweating like a pig about to be stuck, I found my focus and kept on hard down the road and knew every scary second of my path.

Knew it even though it was the death carnival come to town. Still coming. So as I caterwauled my way out of Marvel I crossed many a cornsilk party making its way in. Some were laughing like it was a true carnival, and others had on hard faces like they were marching to war. Some didn't have on any expression at all, like they were killed folk had clawed themselves out of the cemetery just to walk into town and look glass-eyed up into the courthouse trees. One of these was a woman in her old years. She had long gray hair been neatly combed and parted in the middle and she was holding a chicken that was turning its head to and fro, making its comb flop this way and that. Another was a seven-foot giant in dull red shirt and dirty suit and still a third was a young mother and her bald children locked in their stride and slow-stepping it down the road. A block or two after this family I crossed what must have been twins for they were dressed alike in homespun country overalls and yellow shirts and had the same big-nostril cornsilk noses and the same long pipes in their mouths. They were walking arm in arm. Almost step by step.

Spotting them — and it didn't matter that I was getting up on seventy miles per hour — of course got me thinking about Hortensia, and about all the other places I thought she'd be and found she wasn't. We had a mother and a father once, Hortensia and I. And then we didn't. Thinking about her and about them, I left Marvel with those boys' white car not a quarter mile in back of me and hit the poor shacks and bent fences of the outskirts and came on a pair of cornroots fighting in some poplar shade by the road.

You can fit a lot of thinking into a few seconds, and so I must have, because I had stopped the car and jumped out with my basket and come walking on up to them fetching out ham sandwiches before the Dictator's dust plume had had a chance to start falling sideways. One of them looked up at me coming over and the other took advantage to hit him what he hoped would be a good one behind the ear. You could see the punch hadn't hit square. If it had, the brawl or whatever it was would have been over. As it was, the one who had been hit cried foul and the other held up his hands to show he was stopping and I stepped forward with my sandwiches.

"You all are hungry, I can see that," I said.

"Who in the jackrabbit hell are you?" said the one who had been hit on the ear.

"I got sandwiches is who I am," I said. "Thought maybe you were dancing like that because you were hungry and didn't have anything worth eating except each other."

It wasn't the best thing I could have come up with but it was what I said and once something is said to strangers what can you do? My hands were still shaking some. I didn't like it but there we went with that too. If they noticed, they didn't say a thing.

"We're having a fight here. We're in the middle of fighting. You're interrupting a whupping is what's happening," said the other. He was tall and had hair came almost down to the middle of his back. I took another step forward and put a tight-wrapped sandwich in his hand.

"But who's whupping and who's getting some more whupping is the question," said the other. He was shorter, had his hair cropped jagged, and was broader by a powerful amount of real estate around the shoulders. He had stayed crouched a little after he had been punched in the ear and before he finished straightening up I had put the other sandwich in his hand.

"They're good sandwiches," I said. "Made them fresh this morning. You like mustard? There's some mustard. Good pickles. I'm not hungry because I just ate an orange."

"An orange? What do you mean, an orange? And what in hell makes you think we're hungry? You think every cornroot whupping on another cornroot you see needs a sandwich?"

"I don't know. I just said that. You want them? You do, they're yours."

They looked at the sandwiches, then at each other, then at me, then we all turned and looked at the road. The cornsilks had come screeching up in their own dust plume and stopped, and it was hard to see as it fell down on top of them how they could breathe. I set my basket down on the ground where I could reach it easy if I had to, but I didn't have to. There was only three cornsilks in the car and I expect every one of us could see straight off that the boys I was with were worth at least a couple of their variety each. And of course I myself was there too. I lifted up one of my hands and saw it had stopped shaking. About goddamn time. Maybe, I thought—and it

189

makes me laugh now to think of it — twice in one day would be the end of it. We stood there and they sat there in their car. Huffing on their dust. Pretty soon I heard unwrapping and then crunching sounds coming from either side of me and looked and saw that the sandwiches were being eaten, the ham further rendered, the pickle slices put to an end. My sandwich eaters looked up at the cornsilks in their car and crunched down hard. One of the cornsilks had some metal pipe and he waved it out the car window. Another, the one had tossed the mop doll up on the Dictator, took a pull on one of Big Bob's bottles and hollered in a whiskey-choked voice, "Give her up!"

"These your friends?" said the tall one without looking at me.

"These are not my friends," I said.

"You the law?" said the other to the cornsilks, then went back to working his teeth on his sandwich.

"Go to hell," said the driver.

"Yes, sir, we'll do that, right quick," said the tall one.

"She tried to run down folks, including us right here, then strung up the state flag," said the one with his piece of metal pipe. He had a reedy voice didn't help put the bark on his claim too well.

"She what?" said the tall one.

"It was a mop," I said nice and loud. "I put a mop in a state-flag dress and gave it a necktie. They were already devil-dancing under a bloody shirt so I thought maybe they needed something else to dance under. These cornsilk pansy flowers took it down and couldn't even hold on to it. I just stole it from them again."

When I said this, both of the cornroot boys laughed good and loud with their mouths wide open and neither one of them smiling, and when they set in to laughing, the driver started to get out of the car and straightaway I walked toward him and straightaway after that both boys set their sandwiches down on the dusty ground and walked toward him behind me. The driver saw all three of us coming and pulled his leg back in and shut his door.

"We'll see you cornflower bitch and cornroot sons-of-bitches later," he said. "We'll make sure they save you and your mamas some space up in the tree."

This set the boys, who had been walking slowly behind me to the car, to running ahead, and it was just about by the hairy skin of their teeth that the cornsilks got their vehicle turned around and gunned off down the dusty road. The two boys came back coughing. I told them with my eyes glued all the time on the vanishing vehicle that I wished I had some water to offer them.

"Water, hell," said the tall one and picked up his sandwich and took a bite and looked carefully over it at me. "Anyway, what were you going to do when you got up on that boy?"

"I was going to hit him. Weren't you?"

"You planned all that, didn't you?" he said.

I gave a smile and kind of waggled my jaw back and forth, then asked him how he liked his sandwich.

They both laughed. They had let some smile onto their faces. I laughed a little too.

"We were hungry, that's true enough even if you didn't mean it, but that's not why we were fighting," said the shorter one, picking up his own sandwich. He had wrists I liked the look of. They were slimmer than it seemed they ought to have been, almost delicate, despite his broad shoulders.

"Then why were you two fighting?" I asked.

They both shrugged. Said something about the hot day. About a nightmare shift they had just pulled over at Fuller's, where they did day labor by the ovens and sometimes worked nights. They said something about the boys in jail the cornsilks were making the neckties for. About how big the moon had been lately. About how they had fought each other plenty in the past. How they had known each other since they were boys. How the world was a mean bastard and seemed most days like something you needed to take a swing at.

We stood silent together a minute, then the shorter one gave out a kind of snort sounded strange after the quiet we had fallen into and said he reckoned I had played a trick on both them and the cornsilks in their car, that it was a good trick and he bet, from looking at me, that there was more where that came from. He had had a smart-as-a-whip aunt named Betty Peconta with the same look in her eye. She'd once tricked a salesman out of a barrel of Swisher Sweets and she had smoked every last one of them too. I told him that I didn't think it had been what you could call a trick, at least not the kind his aunt had played, and the taller one agreed with me that you wouldn't call it a trick; it had been more of a strategy. Trick or strategy, said the shorter, it didn't matter: I was here talking pleasant in the shade and not getting beat with a pipe or who knows what. He said it paid sometimes to be clever in this world, and I said not enough, it didn't, and they both nodded their heads.

"Did you really eat an orange today?" asked the taller one.

"I did. Still have some of the taste in my mouth."

"I had an orange once. Up in Wabash. Only it was kind of dried out. Was this one dried out?"

I shook my head.

"She doesn't want to talk about oranges," said the shorter one.

"Maybe she does. How in hell do you know?"

I said it was true that I didn't. That it had been delicious and I didn't know what else to say.

"Delicious is saying something," said the shorter one. "Delicious is plenty."

Delicious it was and delicious is plenty, I thought. I asked them their names and the taller one said, "Ben Able," and the shorter one said, "Robert True." I told them my name was Calla Destry and that I lived over on the east side and maybe would still live there again after lynching day had done dug its graves. I thanked them both, then told Ben Able he needed to shift his weight and cock his right hip when he threw his hook, demonstrated what I meant, had Robert True hold up his hand and punched hard into it, smiled when he said I hit harder than Ben Able, which I don't doubt was accurate, picked up my basket, said I was glad they had enjoyed their sandwiches and asked them if now I could give either one or both of them a ride.

Ben Able said they were heading not too many miles down the road, that they had a place in mind where they could wait out the day and the night too if it came to that. I said I thought it would come to that and they nodded and Robert True said if I didn't mind maybe they could ride on the running boards until we came to their turnoff. I said I didn't mind, that good old-fashioned gallants like they were could ride inside the car or out of it. Out of it, they said. And you can just slow down a speck when we get to the turnoff and we'll jump off and be just fine.

So we went over to the car and after they had taken a good long look at the mop doll on the front seat, I climbed in and they climbed on, crouching and holding on to the spare tires and we started down the road. We went by fencerows and barns and shacks and some underfed cows rooting in a mud puddle like pigs. We were pluming up plenty for a while then we hit good blacktop and the pluming stopped and we passed a great yellow swath of honeysuckle and I breathed deep and sped up and Ben Able smiled a set of pretty white teeth in the window at me, and Robert True, his long hair streaming behind him, did the same, then tapped and made a gesture I should roll the passenger window down. I leaned over and did this and he smiled again and reached in and grabbed up that mop doll and yanked it out the window and for a second I thought he was going to throw it into the ditch. Instead he held it out up next to him and hollered and Ben Able pounded on the roof of the Dictator and hollered too.

There's a mind made for magic in there," my Leander said to me once as we were resting one next to the other by his pond. I had come to see him as I always came, after dark in the borrowed Dictator, after we had done one of our nighttime drives and I had left Aunt V and Uncle D and Hortensia back at home.

"What kind of magic?" I said.

He took my hand and kissed it, then kissed it again and said, "The world-whipping kind."

Only kind of whipping I had ever thought about giving the world before I met Leander was the fist variety, the variety Ben Able and Robert True had been talking about, the Roscoe kind. Roscoe had called me over after he saw me palm-smack a boy bigger than I was for making fun of me about Hortensia. I had smacked the boy hard enough to make him take three steps back and I would have smacked him again only Roscoe had me come over and straightaway asked me if I wanted to run with him. And we did. To trouble and away from it. Leander said he liked a girl could hit hard and think smart both. Said that as far as he was concerned there wasn't any kind of girl in the world better than that. Roscoe would have laughed at me about my hands shaking, but he had liked having me run with him and it was him had taught me to stop palm-smacking and to punch.

Aunt V had watched me punch a great big cornsilk girl had made some remark about the color of my hat ribbons on market day not long after they had fetched me past all hope from the orphan house. I had punched her hard in the mouth and the great big girl had gone down on one knee. I would have punched her again like Roscoe always told me I should if they kept talking, and that great big girl had kept talking, but Aunt V had grabbed my arm and hauled me away.

"But that's how you do it," I said.

"And you're lucky she's cornsilk garbage and by her lonesome," Aunt V said. "You're done with doing things that way."

Uncle D felt just the same. So when Roscoe had come up from Indianapolis to see me not long after I had put that girl-giant onto her knee, Uncle D met him at the door with his service revolver. Roscoe had started in right away to talking his fat-fist sauce and calling Uncle D "old man" and "Grandpa," and Uncle D, showing no signs of weak eyes or any of his big smile I already loved so much, had put his gun in Roscoe's face and then, when Roscoe still hadn't shut up, he carefully, slowly, lifted his gun and fired a round into the doorjamb about an inch above Roscoe's head. Roscoe didn't come back for a while and I did get done dropping cornsilk girls after that. So done it wasn't long before I had a job selling flowers around town. And not much more than an inch after I started that job I sold a flower to a man calling himself Leander.

So that even as I joined in the hollering and went fast down that road with Ben Able and Robert True, Leander was wiggle-dancing in front of my eyes and singing out the things like I had magic in my head that he was always saying to me and that I had hoped he would say to me down at the river that morning but he hadn't because he hadn't come. And maybe that was because it was lynching day and maybe it wasn't. Either way I didn't give much more than a tinker's nod when first Ben Able tapped on the window and then Robert True called out that their turnoff was just up ahead. It was only after I slowed down and Robert True handed the mop doll back in and they jumped off at the mouth of a dirt lane went twisting back into a barley field that I thought to wave. Only I didn't know if they saw me do it. And I was thinking about slowing down and maybe even turning around to give them a better fare-thee-well when about that time appeared in my rearview mirror a vehicle of some stripe or other and I thought maybe it was those sorry cornsilks come back with friends. So I hollered out a good-bye even though there wasn't anything outside the car but the corn now to hear. The corn close everywhere around me as I brought the Dictator back up to speed.

Leander; Roscoe; Hortensia; our parents, who'd died in a laundry-house fire...it was the fuel gauge on the Dictator brought me out of my reveries. I had been rolling south and west, set on my idea of what I was going to do, when I hit a hard bump on the road and my eyes flicked up, then down, and I saw what I should have seen ten miles before. I gave a good swallow at the way the fuel dial was pointing to empty and even pulled over a minute next to some wild white hydrangea to think.

'Course there wasn't any thinking to it, just some figuring, so I picked up the mop doll and threw her onto the backseat and took off my hat and slipped out the dollar bill I kept tucked moist inside it under the label. I set the dollar on the seat under my leg then reached into the basket and pulled out the gun. The safety was on so I tugged it off and put it back in the basket. Then I put my hat back on and drove three miles east and two miles north and pulled up under the shiny orange signs of the Gulf station outside Elizaburg. We had driven past it plenty was the time late at night when the lights were turned off and all was quiet. Uncle D kept fuel cans in the shed. Filled them at a cornflower-friendly station in town.

Had stories he didn't like to tell about cornflowers and corn-tassels and cornroots running low on gas when they were out in cornsilk country. Stories that ended badly. That was our style of story in those days. Which hasn't changed. Not near enough. There I was and there you go.

I had barely got the Dictator turned off and the engine still ticking loud when the attendant came quick out of the building and started wiping at my windshield with his rag. He wiped awhile and even started talking about how much bug splatter there had been on the roads lately and how thick the sweat bees had been and how much we needed rain and what he had had for his lunch, and I kept my head down low under my hat. The while of wiping was over quick enough, though, and he came around to my window still talking about sweat bees and sure enough some were landing on his hairy forearm even as he talked about them, digging in down at the loud arm glisten and sucking it up with their face straws.

While he wiped and talked, an old woman came out of the building behind him and sat herself down at a bench by the door. She was dressed in blue calico and scuffed black shoes and didn't have any teeth. I looked sideways at her, and the attendant went around to the back of the Dictator and started pumping and while he pumped did some more wiping at the back window with his free hand. He had set aside the talking and was whistling now. He wasn't a bad whistler. He was well into his middle years and had a gut on him bulged out of his beige work shirt that looked like it contained a fine-size pig.

He finished his pumping and started back around to my window, and as he came around the old lady leaned forward, looked hard at me, and said, "Goddamn, boy, that child in there you're pumping gas for is a cornflower."

She croaked this out and, flash-quick, the attendant's greasy forearm and those sweat bees had been on it got fused in my mind. I saw that arm flying in with yellow wings through the window and grabbing at me and yanking me off my seat and into the station where it would beat on me until I was just a pile of mash then leave me to the old lady, who would sweep me up and throw me out with the garbage.

As he came up to the window I pulled the gun out of the basket and held it in my lap. If he saw it I didn't know straightaway because what he said next, and he looked me square in the eye when he said it, was "Fifty cents, please."

I looked at him and he looked at me.

"Fifty cents, that's it?" I said.

"Yes, miss, we don't try to take advantage here."

"That's a goddamn cornflower, Erastus!" the old woman said. She had leaned back against the wall of the station. Her words came out flabby because there wasn't any teeth to help them. Aunt V had trouble with her teeth. She worked on them every day with Colgate powder. Made all of us work on ours too.

"Be still now, Mama, I'm with a customer here," said the attendant.

I had left the gun in my lap and taken the dollar bill out

from under my leg. When the attendant took it from me, our fingers touched a little and he said excuse me. There were three sweat bees working an angry scrape on his forearm. Others hovering in the air. I tipped him ten cents.

"You come back here anytime now, miss," he said. "It's a damn awful shame," he continued after a pause.

"Yes, sir."

"I'm no *sir*. I'm Erastus Fellows and go to Quaker meetings and that old lady on the bench wishing you bad luck is my mother and she doesn't go. It isn't every bone in her body is evil. Just the majority of them."

"I can hear you. I can hear every word," the old lady said.

"I know it, Mama. I know you can. And yet here I stand, still speaking."

He tipped his hat at me and said, in a lower voice, that setting the Quaker ways he believed in aside, I was wise on a day as bad as this one to carry a gun, that I should keep my eyes open and watch careful where I stopped. What was happening in Marvel wasn't right but it was happening, and I had to look careful.

"It's just plain wrong," he finally said.

"Wrong?" I said.

He had a little smile on his face now was probably meant nothing but kindly and his forearm didn't look like any monster sweat bee and his little eyes were bright. He nodded and gave the window frame of the Dictator a sloppy pat then stepped away. And here is the second funny thing that happened in my head while I was at the Gulf station in Elizaburg on that lynching day. Even if it was him being kind and his mother over on her bench gumming out hate, the truth is if I had been out of the car and had my feet under me, I would have hit him, not his mother, then hit him again, then done a dance and stamped him into the ground. I would have stamped him and his kindly words and his "Fifty cents, please" into the ground. Then thrown salt and lime powder onto what was left. Then I would have spat into the lime powder and watched my spit sizzle. Then let the old lady toss *him* out with the trash.

Wrong wasn't the word for what was happening. It was a thousand miles from what needed saying. There wasn't any word on the earth a cornsilk could say and make it sound right and so what a cornsilk needed to do was just keep his kindly mouth stapled shut. Even this sweet fat Erastus Fellows who had maybe never hurt a fly or a sweat bee and pumped his gas for all.

I had the gun in my lap and now my hand went back around it. I could shoot him and let his old mother, who at least said what she thought, gum out a few last words over his body. Maybe I could get out and hit him first. Lord, I could hit hard. Robert True had said it, and Roscoe couldn't give a fig about me and my mind magic, but he had made me his lieutenant. A few good punches, then *blam!* And maybe one right now. Right now out the car window. All this came upon me so quickly I had to take a deep breath and shut my eyes and let my traitor hands that had started into shaking again go limp to push it back down. When they were open again, I thanked him and left the gun in my lap and started the Dictator and drove away.

I'd meant to head straight on down west and south again and get to where I knew now for sure I was going, but what I did once I was out of Elizaburg and into the countryside was stop and get out of the Dictator and scream. I screamed, then pounded on the passenger-side spare tire of the Dictator, and then yanked the mop doll out of the car and smacked it over and over again against the ground and then against a tree. When I was done smacking I pulled myself and it up onto one of the lower branches and found that once I had started climbing I couldn't stop, even holding on to that mop doll. I got up to a high branch, screamed again, then thought about the boys in jail or already out of it and I tied mop doll up and let her hang and I liked letting her hang instead of those boys something fierce.

I watched her hang awhile, twisting this way and that, and felt my breathing settle. It was an oak tree I was in. Strong. The leaves fluttered dark and full in the hot air of the afternoon. I saw my hands had calmed some and seeing that made me breathe even more easy and looking at her and feeling calm and breathing more easy and seeing out over the fields I realized I was thinking about that piece of butcher paper on

Big Bob's desk. His map picture had dribbles of whiskey on it. Pot of silver paint. Getting ready for its frame of pictures. Garland of cornflowers. Land below could use some whiskey on it. Drops to settle it down. Calm its creeks. Cool its lanes. Suck out all its slivers. Quench its thirsts. Catch a spark and set it aflame. I looked out and let my eyes trace along the field edges with silver. Cobwebs across the shivery corn. Big Bob had written *Marvel* at the middle of his page. So I knew since I was already miles from Marvel that I was somewhere out on its edges. Maybe part of that frame he was planning to make. All of us one after the other out on its edges. None of us knowing just what we were looking at.

"Wrong," I said. I said it thinking about Erastus Fellows but also because I didn't know what Big Bob's picture map was for. How could I know? He hadn't said and I'd barely seen. I said "Wrong" and wished Hortensia was there and felt emptied out and didn't think about shooting anyone anymore. Just thought about Big Bob's shop and the quiet there and the map picture lying on his desk in the cool dark.

"Oh, Calla," Hortensia had said. The last time I had seen her. The last time I saw her. Five years, it was. Couple of happy young fools playing dolls and trying to teach ourselves the "Wang Wang Blues." Sitting there in the front yard of the orphan house. Put that on Big Bob's map. Day a cornsilk couple had come and had us run races together and climb trees just like this one and even swim in the White River then had talked about how light-skinned we both were and what a marvel that was, especially Hortensia, and you could hardly tell and we had both smiled because we were young and stupid and then they had showed us how they only had one spot in their Ford and then they had told us their choice and then they had taken her off with them forever.

We had been swimming in the White River and she was gone before our hair was dry. "Oh, Calla," she had said and I hadn't said anything and you tell me what kind of story that is and then she had climbed in their car.

Didn't make any difference that about a week later she was back. Back to climb trees with me and swim and kick at me in our bed and sing the "Wang Wang Blues" when we woke up. Didn't matter that I was the only one could see and hear her. Or that she wasn't there all the time. That she would leave me for long stretches. Go out and walk. Visit other states. See the world, learn its ways. Now there was the map I wanted. One that would show me where she was walking, where all the others who had left me had gone, where I should go.

We hadn't seen them coming, that cornsilk couple. Suddenly they had just been there, like smiling monsters in a story, and we went running and splashing around all day like slit-throat ducks. Matron at the orphan house said afterward she didn't know where they had taken Hortensia. That there wasn't any way to know. That it didn't matter how many times I asked her. That I should sit back down and eat my supper and be happy for her and stop pretending she was sitting in her seat next to me and "Goddamn it, Calla Destry, be still!"

You don't have the map, you need eyes, I thought. *You need about a hundred out here if you want to catch it all. Catch it all and not get caught.* The way Hortensia had been. Gobbled up by the smiling monsters. I got down out of the tree, brushing on the dark green oak leaves as I went, and it was when I stopped my glance on the dent that little girl had made in the Dictator's driver's-side door that I saw it. Plucked it up out of my magic mind. Uncle D kept some of his lettering paints and brushes bagged up tight in the Dictator's trunk, said it was his storage shelf, kept the tools of his trade safe and serene. The Dictator was sitting in the oak shade and the metal had started to cool. I emptied the jars of paint onto its backseat, picked out the ones I liked, unscrewed their lids, chose a brush, started with the little girl's dent, drew a almond shape around it. Made eyelashes on the almond. Thought about Big Bob's map. Colored in the middle where the metal had shown through. The paint trickled here and there but I dipped my brush light and mostly it held.

"Eyes all over," I said. I let myself imagine that Uncle D was there nodding and watching me work. That Aunt V was sitting over by the tree fanning herself. That Hortensia in her blue hat was laughing at my latest notion. That even Roscoe was there. Arms folded over his chest. Big Bob and his little dog, Myrtle, too. They were the frame for my map. We had all driven out of Marvel together. Maybe stopped on our way out at the Handy Brothers for cold soda pop. Hortensia's favorite had been orange cream. Lord, I wished I could have shared my part of Big Bob's orange with her. How she would have clapped her hands. Maybe wherever she was, she was eating oranges. Pineapples and lemons too.

I could see mop doll hanging way up in the branches and suddenly felt sad for her. Shouldn't be anything hanging on this day. I brought her back down and leaned her against the trunk and put a pair of eyes on her mop fringe with red paint and talked to her and to myself as I worked on the Dictator. "Don't you leave this beauty with any blind spots. I want it to see everything. Everything, now. Everywhere. No more surprises, all right?"

When I was done I screwed the lids back on the paint, left them sitting on the backseat, walked over to the tree and stood by mop doll and told her that the Dictator had never looked more beautiful and that I thought sure Uncle D would agree. My hands were covered in paint so I wiped them on the ends of mop doll's dirty fringe. She looked good with red and green and blue and gold at the ends of her hair. "You look good," I said. I told her we had to go. To Ryansville. Where Leander lived.

I had seen him in the daylight only once before, that very first time. Taking his jelly-bread stride across the courtyard square. I was helping sell flowers by the diner. He came over, bought a rose, gave me a wink, and whispered would I meet him that very night in the alley behind the bank for he had matters of gravest import to discuss. I laughed at the silly sound of his voice and even sillier words but I met him. I told him my name was Calla Destry, and he said I was the most beautiful young woman he had ever seen, that I was more beautiful than any woman who had ever appeared in any of his dreams or in the dreams of any others since the world was made. Then he took his hand out from behind his back where he had been hiding it and produced the flower he had bought from me earlier. The flower was wilted plenty and I already knew it didn't have any smell. But apart from Roscoe once tearing me up some narcissus and tossing them to me as we got up to no good near the White River not one week before Aunt V and Uncle D came to the orphan house to offer me a spot in their vehicle, it was the first time anyone had ever given me a flower. Leander might have tried to kiss me on that first night and I surely would have let him only a gang of cornsilk boys started kicking at empty boxes down the alley and Leander gave me a bow, told me to meet him again the next week, and off he went running.

The next week he did kiss me. His mouth tasted like violet candy. I put my hand a minute on his waist and found it soft as an uncooked snickerdoodle. When it came time to part our ways he started in to fretting because he had just sold his father's Ford and wouldn't be able to easily get back to see me. He had sold it, he told me, upon his father's death and with his mother's accord, so that he could use the proceeds to further his political ambitions. "I will be governor someday," he said. It was a strange thing to say in an alley after dark in the middle of some sweet kissing and we both laughed a little. He had a pretty laugh. Higher and finer than his voice. Roscoe did not have a pretty laugh. Roscoe was just a boy not much older than I was, but he already had a laugh that croaked doom, like a frog swallowed by a cat swallowed by a wolf eaten up ugly by a bear. I got beat down by another girl in an alley when I was still learning how to swing and Roscoe laughed his laugh at me instead of helping me up. He would have laughed it long and hard to see me selling flowers. I told Leander about our yellow beast, our Dictator, hiding under its shroud, in our shed, behind my new home. I told him, and my visits to see him commenced. And here on a day of mobs and murder I went driving with my mop and basket and car covered in eyes and Uncle D's paint jars rattling on the backseat towards another visit.

So and despite all, up and out of my chest my heart flew, racing ahead of the Dictator, rising fast for Ryansville, leaving my body feeling slow and faint and oh so small behind me. Small is how I felt when I got there anyway. Small, and stupid too; I was happy enough to have put eyes on the car and the mop when I was out in the country, but I found I didn't like the idea any too much, when I got to Ryansville, of sailing through the streets with my companion in that bright eyeball-covered machine. The world is full of rocks. And full of rope. Which is saying I had a thought as my heart fell hard out of the sky and down my throat and back into my chest about turning around and heading straight for Big Bob's fishing spot. Skip the mobs. Skip the murder. Wait for dark to make my visit. I took the thought so far I slowed the Dictator down at a four-way stop near the lane that led to Leander's, and, fool that I was, I then found a way to stall it.

Matron had had a stereoscope at the orphan house in Indianapolis I was allowed to look through sometimes. Most of the cards she had were of cornsilk children and cornsilk grown-ups with not a cornflower anywhere to be found; state of the world and nothing special. She had one stack of cards, though, that was just landscapes and buildings and monuments didn't have in them any people of any variety at all. And those were the cards I loved. Because without anyone in them I could imagine they were full of cornflowers. Cornflowers by the hundreds, hiding behind trees, behind doors, waiting to push up windows and holler out as I looked in. I wanted more than anything else in the world after Hortensia left to live in there with them. Sometimes I thought I heard a familiar cough or a laugh come from just around one of the quiet corners and did all I could to pour myself out of my eyes and onto that street or empty forest glade. One time, after I had described it to him, Roscoe came to see me late into the small hours and we sneaked into Matron's office and studied up on those stereoscope pictures by lamplight.

"We're in there," Roscoe had said, taking to the idea straightaway. "That's you and me just down at the end of the street past those rail tracks. That's us swimming just below the surface of the lake. We're everywhere," he said. "What about Hortensia?" I said. "She's in there too. Hell yes, she is. We're all up there in the clouds. Beyond the banks of the river. On top of those pyramids. On our thrones in that palace. You can see us in that woods, look close now, that's us hiding behind the trunks of those trees."

And for a strange minute that early August evening — with the Dictator's engine ticking towards quiet, and a cardinal calling down the street — cornsilk Ryansville had some of that feeling for me. World emptied out and ready for other feet to be the ones to walk its roads. Other faces to answer its doors. To tend its shops. To honk its horns and light its lights. Still, pretty dreams of a moment put aside, I wasn't ignorant, wasn't dumb. I knew it was a cornsilk had taken those pictures of empty landscapes and that it was cornsilks had built every inch of what I was looking at now. If there was anyone hiding behind Ryansville's trees or waiting quiet behind its curtains, it wasn't cornflowers. That was for sure. And when I had had that thought I had another I didn't like as I looked around the Dictator at the empty streets. *They've got one going over here too* is what I thought.

Any fool wasn't me would have flown back on out of Ryansville then, would have found Big Bob, who had been kind to me, or turned my searching to Aunt V and Uncle D, who had both that morning shook their heads as they looked my way, shook them slow and long as I walked out their door, but instead I started the Dictator back up, drove it off behind a derelict shed had been covered up into a cave by vines and shrub trees, made sure I did a better job hiding it this time, grabbed my basket, and got out. Left mop doll sit there with the jars of paint to keep her company. Started stepping forward, not even sure what I was walking toward. It was like the silence had a smell. The emptiness a taste. I made my hands into fists that felt good even if it was just to keep them from shaking. Calla Destry—the version of her that made fists and went forward and didn't fear.

I found the good people of Ryansville gathered outside the Methodist church. I didn't see any bloody shirt but that didn't mean there wasn't one. They were smiling and nodding their heads and murmuring "Yes" and "That's right" and "Uh-huh." Some of them turned and saw me come up but if one of them did raise his eyebrow at the sight of me, that was the worst I got. I went on and even stepped up among them and ready now to unfist my hand and fetch what was in my basket, but when I got up close enough I saw I wasn't going to have to because it wasn't any boy or girl up a tree they were attending to. They hadn't caught themselves any cornflowers. Unless, of course, they had just been waiting, spidery, for the right fly to come along. I took a step more and got a smile out of a nearby heavy lady who was sweating even worse than all the rest of us. Sweating so much the edge of her yellow hat brim was wet. A smile from a lady. They didn't want to lynch me.

I breathed out and felt my mind relax for it was just a group of cornsilks entertaining themselves on a summer afternoon. Just people maybe like that Erastus Fellows but in Sunday suits and clean overalls and pretty dresses. I couldn't see him yet but he was loud, this speaker they had. A great booming voice to break through the crickets and cicadas sawing it up everywhere around us. A voice coming to the close of its orations. Talking about supper to be eaten, then buses to be boarded and a noble journey to be made and a Christian and patriotic mission to be fulfilled. I shivered and thought, *Wrong,* and my head spun and the fat woman smiled at me once more and I looked slowly from her over to the speaker and as my eyes traveled the voice stopped booming and grew softer a moment, soft and tender for that second, and in that second before my eyes had completed their journey I knew whose voice it was.

As soon as Leander had stopped his speaking, the whole crowd gave up a last hurrah and went heading hard for the church doors. They went in one great, sweat-soaked rush, saying things about catfish and cornbread and getting a good place on some buses when the buses got there. They went so hard and fast that a minute later there wasn't anyone left in the churchyard except Leander, who had his handkerchief out and was wiping with it at his forehead. I had been standing just at the edge of a great tall rose of Sharon and started to step toward him, so he could see me and I could call him over, and he could tell me what all this meant and why in hell he hadn't come to see me by the river that morning, not to mention what all this talk about buses and righteous missions was, but as I started forward I saw a woman come up out of the church carrying a plate loaded with food. She set her plate down at a table and presently my sweet Leander skipped on over.

She looked to me, did this woman, like she was worth about two cents and some old turkey feathers, but my Leander who hadn't come to see me that morning headed straight on over to her. Just about flew his way over, though you could see even fifty feet off that she didn't have any interest in talking to him, least not with her plate piled high in front of her. Leander was dressed in a suit I hadn't seen before. It didn't fit him worth a dog catcher's curse and his hairpiece had come loose a touch. He put his hand on his hip and started talking and the lady answering. She had on a tight green dress and blue shoes. She had what you might call a button nose and a great big chest. Her hat could have used some adjustment; a couple sharp sprigs of long red hair had sprung loose.

While Leander leaned over this lady, the horde started percolating back up from the church with their own plates piled high. Looking at those plates, and now the lovely clean-fried smell of fish swimming over at me, I realized that the only thing I had eaten since a couple of Aunt V's flapjacks early that morning was Big Bob's special orange, which had sat like Shangri-La in my mouth and nothing in my belly. I thought this and heard my stomach grumble and then that heavy lady who had smiled at me a few minutes before came out of the church with two plates. It took her a long time to get to me since she walked slow and stopped to talk at every table. But get to me she did.

"Here you go, doll," she said. "This is God's food and made to be eaten by all."

"By all—you sure about that, ma'am?" I said.

"Go on, now, it's good. I know the girls who cooked it. One of them is aunt to that fine speaker we just heard. I came all the way over from Forrest to hear him. I saw you got there at the end but he could really hit the high notes. He's going somewhere. You can see it a mile off."

She laughed and we both looked over at Leander. He had just left off talking to the red-haired woman and was making for the church doors.

"His aunt cooked this?" I said.

"She's a sweet one, just like he is."

"What about his mother, did she help?"

"His mother? Say, honey, did you bring something for the supper?" She was looking at my basket. " 'Cause if you did I could take it down for you."

I looked at the basket, then at her, then had to bite at the inside of my lip not to laugh at the image of the heavy lady taking out the gun and laying it down in the church basement with the catfish and casseroles.

"Did he really make a good speech?" I said, biting even harder and getting the better of myself.

"I thought it was about the best I ever heard. Church and country. Got in some mentions of wildlife. Wildfire too! And then all this talk about highways, lanes, and thoroughfares."

I didn't know what else to say so I just said, "That sounds fine."

"You enjoy that now, doll, and aren't you the handsomest thing," she said. "You remind me of a girl we once had to work in our kitchen. Only you're a little lighter-skinned."

I told her I wasn't even allowed into the kitchen at home. This was true. I had cooked some back at the orphan house but had burned up the three things I had tried in Aunt V's kitchen and been banished.

"Enjoy and remember," she said. "It ain't nothing but good Christian folks here, even if there is a few bad ones. There's always a few bad ones in every bunch!" She gave out a wink and a cackle like there was something extra about what she had said that I was supposed to understand and she walked off with her own plate. I stood there and watched her walk, her legs so thick you couldn't be sure she was making them bend, then, fierce hungry as I was, I took the catfish she had given me and tossed it deep into the rose of Sharon.

While I had talked to the nice Christian lady who believed I looked like her kitchen helper, Leander had come back out of the church, flitted here and there between the tables, then flew off. So I got the thought in my head that maybe now with his speech done and his supper eaten he would be on his way home and reckoned his home would be as good a place as any other to have our talk. We needed to have our talk. It couldn't wait. I straightened up and smoothed the front of my dress, started to leave, maybe get there first, catch him on the lane that led up to the house. Have our talk somewhere off away from his mother. Not disturb her. Keep it quiet. Quiet as what I had to say and how he would answer would let me be.

But then I heard a rumbling and looked out through the leaves and pink Sharon roses to the road. As I watched, a line of five fresh-painted lily-white buses pulled up. My Leander was behind the wheel of the first one. He gave its horn a few good honks then leaned out the door and hollered, loud enough so that even I could hear it, far enough away as I already was, "Anyone ready to get on the road to Marvel and join the party, climb aboard!"

There are times I sit here and think on it—and thinking on it is practically all I do—that the sky goes cloudy and black behind Leander and those buses. It's not every time and not pitch-black like it is with the courthouse. I don't float up out of my hiding place behind the rose of Sharon and fly over into the buses and swirl around in the seats. It's more like a quick cloud or a chunk of moon or a careless devil's thumb covering over the sun. Covering up my walking quickly away from that churchyard. It all smears dark a little but then it lights up again.

There were some smart-looking starlings pecking at the vines next to the Dictator and two or three of them hopping around on its hood. They scattered when I came up and joined a greater, louder group ganged up by the dozen in the branches of a nearby catalpa tree. Roscoe had never liked starlings. Said that smart little look made his neck hair stand on end. Gave him nightmares if they kept it on him too long. I didn't like any kind of bird when it was gathered in great number but I had otherwise always thought starlings looked handsome. When I shut the Dictator's door, a few of them jumped up from their branch, and when I started the engine they all lifted up like one thing and wheeled away. I asked mop doll what she thought of the birds and she stared straight ahead. Had the focus I was looking for. I could see when I got the Dictator out of its hiding place and back on the road that the buses were about ready to roll.

Considerable cheering came out the polished windows, clenched fists were raised, honking cars had lined up behind. I thought I could see the heavy lady had tried to feed me that pile of food. Food for all. Catfish of the Lord. I had been to church plenty. I had heard the good message. The Klan were honest churchgoers wanted what was best for their country, and cornflowers and anything wasn't silk came straight from the devil, and we all needed to work hard and never speak, and Jesus Christ was a carpenter who conjured miracle fish for cornsilks to gobble. So forth and so on.

There was a side lane went past cowsheds that I knew would take me out of town then loop me back around. I'd used it before. Do it quick and have a talk with my sweet Leander after all. The cows were all huddled up in their sheds. I gave them an extra dust blanket when I went past.

"You ready now, girl?" I said and the mop doll wouldn't answer, so I answered for her.

"Yes," I said.

I wasn't more than a hundred yards out when the first bus, Leander's, started in to honking at me. Leander was waving his hand crazy like there was a hornet behind the windshield and about half the riders had their heads out the windows and were waving at the air like they thought that might work some miracle and make me turn. I've already said the Dictator could fly when you wanted it to. Fly, straight toward those buses, we did. It was me flying ahead of my heart this time. My car, covered in angry eyes. My heart, back in the churchyard. I would feel this true.

For a long second I thought that at least one of us was going to keep driving, and driving straight, that right out there in the middle of the hot road we would have ourselves a kiss, only a lot bigger and louder than the one I had been imagining us having all day. The one after I had told him what I had to tell him and he had answered right. Kiss like the kinds Roscoe had always given me. Like all that mattered was the kiss. All those kisses. Kisses that didn't stop after Uncle D had put the bullet in the doorjamb. Kisses that didn't stop even after Leander had commenced his courting, after I had told him, Roscoe, thinking I meant it, that we were through.

But I saw Leander slowing so I slowed, and then Leander stopped and I stopped. We both kept our vehicles running. I watched him turn and tell the people in the bus to hold tight, that he would attend to the impediment before him. He did the same thing again when he stepped out of the bus, for the drivers behind him had all come down out of their own conveyances. He paused a minute to gather himself when he had turned back toward me. He straightened his tie, smoothed his suit, and wiggled his jaw. While he was flattening down his hairpiece I rose from the Dictator, leaving the basket, and came and stood in front of the vehicle with my arms crossed.

"Sweet Jesus on Sunday morning, Calla!" he said when he saw it was me. "You gave me a scare. What in God's name are you doing here? You have sprung up out of the earth like a phantom. What has happened to the Dictator? Why is it covered in eyes?"

He took a step closer. The crowd had grown and was shifting behind him. He looked over his shoulder, called out, "It's all right, folks," and turned back to me.

"Calla, Calla, my darling, you have to leave, this isn't the time for us to meet, truly, it isn't."

"You didn't come this morning," I said. "I sent you a message to come."

"What message? Come where?"

"I waited. I brought us a picnic. I had something to tell you. I still do."

"What in hell, Hale?" said a bulky man wearing a driver's cap coming up behind him.

"It's all right, it's all right," said Leander. "It's a young woman on the road, Morely. I think she is unwell. I will help her and we will be on our way. Don't come too close. Let's not scare her. I think she may be lost."

I cocked my head but otherwise didn't move. Morely looked dubious and spit a squirt of chaw out the side of his mouth. Five or six others had come up to stand beside him.

Some of the people I'd noticed at the church. I looked to see if the heavy lady or the red-haired woman or maybe even Leander's mother was in their number, but they weren't. Leander came another step closer.

"You don't mind that I've called you unwell or lost, do you, my sweet? I said it to throw them off. To keep our secret." He whispered this last part and kept looking over his shoulder, then back at me. He gave out a small and nervous laugh. His fingers were twitching and turning at his sides like little pond eels.

"Pick up that crazy cornflower bitch and toss her in the corn!" called a woman's voice. I couldn't see where she was standing. Most of the men had straw toppers pulled low over their brows. The women's faces were lost under fruit- and flower-smothered hats. Quite a little crowd had gathered. There was considerable snickering and laughing. I spotted the heavy lady. She was pointing at me and talking into the ear of an old fellow, might have been her husband, who was standing next to her.

"My darling Calla, *please*..." said Leander. His eyes had the look in them like they got when he wanted me to do something. Something private. "Can't we speak about this later, perhaps tonight upon my return? You could just back the Dictator up to that tractor lane over there yonder and turn it around. The road is too narrow and the ditches too deep for us to safely pass you."

"Do you mean upon your return from Marvel and having

missed our rendezvous and tête-à-tête this morning, you imagine we could converse at our leisure and in appropriate intimacy in your nearby place of dwelling, Mr. Homer Hale of Ryansville?" I said. I said it loud, and he flinched so hard when I said *appropriate* and *intimacy* and *dwelling* that I thought he would fall over backward and knock down some of his friends.

"Not so loud, *please*, Calla, please, my darling," Leander whispered. He went from flinching back to moving even closer to me just about without my noticing it. His hair had come good and cockeyed again and his belly fat was spilling a little out of his shirt where a button had sprung loose. He looked over his shoulder to the crowd that had come in closer with him. "Just one more minute, my good people, and we will have her on her way, she has taken too much heat, as probably we all have," he said. He pulled out his handkerchief and patted at his head. I saw now it was a light blue handkerchief trimmed about its edges with purple carnations. I had given it to him the last time we met. Bought it with money I had stolen out of Aunt V's purse. I do not know if he realized which handkerchief it was, not when he was patting his brow, nor when he held the dampened thing out to me and asked me if I would care to make use of it. Both of us looked at the handkerchief. Probably everyone who was standing there did.

"No, thank you, Mr. Hale, though that is a pretty handkerchief you are offering me."

Someone called out about getting the buses rolling even if

227

they had to roll over me and my car. Leander put the handkerchief back into his pocket, leaned in close, and put his mouth almost next to my ear. "I have rented these machines at some good expense, both to me and to my mother," he said. He leaned in a little closer. "I have incurred debt for them. It is for my career. All of this. That is all." Even closer. "For our future, *our* future, my love."

I leaned in then too, put my lips to his ear, whispered, "Where is your new friend in the green dress, Mr. Hale?"

"What friend?"

"The blowsy bitch with the red hair," I hissed.

"I don't understand, Calla, were you there, at the supper? Where have you come from? What's all this about a picnic? I don't understand anything." As he said this his voice rose and he grabbed a little at the sleeve of my dress.

"Please step away from me now, Mr. Hale," I told him, my voice bright and firm again. "You are standing too close."

He did as I said. He did it uncomfortably but gracefully, and made a little bow.

When he was away from me I pulled back my shoulders and said, "Are you driving these folks to Marvel to see the lynching of those young cornflower boys, Mr. Hale?" I spoke even louder than I had before and there was a murmuring in the crowd. It rippled forward and back. I thought about those starlings, swooping in their shivering rush through the air. *You aren't anything near as nice to look at as Roscoe,* I thought, looking at Leander, standing there sweating and spilling out of his shirt. He was moving those long fingers of his. Slower now, like he did when he was thinking. I didn't let him finish his thought.

"I am pregnant," I said.

Leander looked at me, took half a step to the side, then stood there struck dumb like he had turned straight to salt and lacked only the cow to come and lick at him.

"I am pregnant," I said again, louder this time.

There was more murmuring from the crowd. The heavy lady edged closer. Morely was playing with his cap.

"We will speak again this evening, Mr. Hale, yes, I like that plan of yours. I very much like it," I said. Then I called out to the crowd, as loudly as I could, "Are all of you bound for Marvel to see the lynching?"

"Hell yes, we are!" is more or less the answer I got. I turned my back on them then, and on Leander, and stepped to the Dictator.

"Calla," Leander said as I climbed in.

"How do you know that young girl's name?" said the heavy lady. "And what did she mean by telling you she's in the family way?"

Leander stood there silent and frozen between me and the heavy lady. And at just that minute came a kind of scraping sound, and an old cornsilk man shuffled up next to the Dictator dragging a big gun.

"Come on back out here and pick this thing all the way up for me so I can fire it at these sons-of-bitches," he said out of the side of his mouth when he was up next to my window.

"Is that crazy old Wilton?" I heard someone say. "He thinks that gun can be shot. It ain't been shot since the Civil War and probably didn't even work then."

"It worked fine then because I killed people like you with it and it works just fine now, you sad sons-of-bitches," said this Wilton, shaking his fist.

There was a gale of laughter. The crowd was already dispersing a little, people going back to their cars and places on the buses. Leander hadn't moved a muscle. His long fingers gleamed and glistened dull now.

"There's more than one way to butcher this hog," I told the old man. "Step to the side and watch yourself, now." Looking into Leander's unmoving eyes, I put the Dictator in reverse.

I looked just once over my shoulder to make sure the way was clear, then turned to face forward, put both my hands on the wheel, and watched a slumped-shoulder Leander and the buses and the cars and the town of Ryansville grow smaller and smaller like a problem that could be solved and made to vanish away forever just by leaving it behind. But there stood Leander. I could not stop looking at him. And it seemed to me even as I rolled backward that there wasn't just relief in the movement that came first to his mouth, then his cheeks, then his fine, wide lips, that there was something else, something softer, tenderer, which I knew I would remember for many a year and that I knew I would be sorry for, just as long, to see leave him, as leave him it did when I hit the Dictator's brake.

Stopped it just far enough back to get a good running start, then set the Dictator to leaping forward as fast as its shiny wheels would go.

I had this idea that just about half the whole world would shake when the Dictator and that bus did have their kiss. As it was, apart from the sound of some of Uncle D's paint jars shattering and some ugly scrape and crunch from the collision, the loudest noise came from the old man, who had somehow got his big gun pointed skyward and pulled the trigger and blasted off a black-powder boom. It was to him dancing and hollering and twirling around that I stepped out of the Dictator when I realized I couldn't back it away, that the grilles of the two vehicles had gotten tangled and stuck. I had hit my head a good one on the steering wheel too and it spun a little as I stood and sniffed at the air and rubbed at some blue paint splotches on my wrist, which was also sore.

Apart from the old man who was dancing his roadside jig, there was a sure silence to the buses and the cars behind them. Like the whole line and all it contained had been turned to salt. Leander, who had jumped out of the way as I drove down on him, was sitting in the side ditch with his elbows on his knees and his handkerchief hanging limp in his hands. The mop doll and picnic basket had gone for their own merry ride with the loose paint around the inside of the car after I had hit the bus, and my hat had come so far loose and had caught so many splotches of color that I tore it the rest of the way off my head and tossed it to the ground.

"You see all that?" I said to them. Then I said it again to the eyes on the Dictator. "You attending to this, little girl?"

Some of those people were starting to stand. There was a man in the front row of Leander's bus holding on to the top of his shoulder like it hurt. Others were climbing down out of the buses behind. Their conveyances were stuck a good while at least behind Uncle D's Dictator and Leander's ruined bus on the narrow road. But *they* weren't stuck and I figured I had about thirty seconds before I became lynching material myself. So I leaned back in the car, grabbed up my poor paint-spattered basket, settled mop doll, eyes facing front and fierce, behind the steering wheel, and turned.

"Good-bye, Homer Hale," I said. "I am sorry to have spoiled your excursion and to have injured your investment. I do hope there is something you can salvage of your day."

"The sheriff will be coming," he said, looking up at me. His hair had come almost entirely off his head and was hanging over one of his ears. He wasn't smiling but he wasn't crying either and I thought I saw a gleam in his eye. "He is riding in the last bus. He is a heavy man and slow to move, but once he gets going, if he can see his target, he doesn't stop."

"I am leaving," I said.

"Is it true?" he said.

I took the pretty handkerchief out of his hands, used it to wipe at the paint on my arms and the back of my neck and on the top of the basket. Then I returned it to him.

"It's true," I said and stepped from him into the thicket of corn. It was eight feet high if it was a inch. Shouts jumped up and I heard some crashing behind me and I was glad I had my sturdy shoes and could run. And, basket in my arms or not, I did. First cutting through the stalks, row after row, pushing away the crispy leaves so I could find my way through, and then, when I was deep into the field, running down the rows, basket held up high to protect my face, and only every thirty strides or so cutting diagonally through the stalks. It could have been a hundred people or not a one after me with those dry leaves whacking my arms and face, I wouldn't have known.

I ran for a long while, catching heavy spiderwebs across my arms and sending big yellow hoppers into the air, ran through loud and quiet, light and shade, then came at last into a clearing of stunted corn. The clearing was big enough to tell me where I was, tell me exactly: not much more than yelling distance from Leander's farm. I heard crashing behind me and plunged back into the tall corn. A few minutes later, I stepped out of the field and alongside a creek. I followed the creek, making little frogs leap into loud rings, and came to Leander's swimming hole, where I'd swam with him many a night.

I ran and kept running but part of me jumped out of myself and into the cool water when I passed that pond. I ran, breathing hard and wrist hurting and head pounding, and that other part of me plunged. Went in fully dressed through the sunlit water, cleaned off paint and sweat, knife-sailed down and dark, deep and fast to the bottom, where I closed my eyes and said to myself, "Sleep now, Calla Destry. Drown."

I don't know if it was the me that was killing herself under the shallow deep or the me that was foot-pounding through the afternoon that realized I wasn't being followed anymore. Either way, soon as I did I sat straight down on the path that led up from the pond to the house and put my face in my hands.

Aunt V, no girl's fool, had yanked me hard aside more than once, that morning included, and told me that whatever it was I didn't think she knew I was doing by carrying on with cornflowers and cornsilks both, it wouldn't end well. "Going to end in torn hair and teardrops" is what she said. About that fine piece of trouble kept coming up from Indianapolis. About that lump of drippy molasses I'd left in the ditch.

And yes, I was crying as I sat there with my face in my hands. I had been crying since I stepped out of the ditch and into the corn. Had been crying as I flew through the cool of the pond water. Crying since those begonias. Since that girl threw that rock. Since Big Bob fed me that orange. Crying all that day. Since I rose from the river. Since I took Uncle D's service revolver and put it in the picnic basket. Since Aunt V had stood next to Uncle D and watched me make ham sandwiches on the back porch and told me I could go straight to the devil if it was the devil I needed so bad to see.

Still, you step on. You're young. You were young once. You are far from your friends. You do. I got up slow, spit hard, ran my hands over my hair, walked fast down the winding lane, and came out into the Hales' yard. Land grant and in their family for eighty-five years. Looking fine for it. The black-eyed Susans were wilty and the red and yellow rosebushes and about all the rest gave the impression they could have used a good long drink, but the grass was mowed neat and the hedges trimmed and the walkways swept clean.

Leander's father had been a farmer of parts, at least for a while, and they had a big white house and a big white barn and other white things built up and fresh-painted all around. The father had had the reins on it right up until he had punched his own exit ticket by swallowing a cupful of carbolic acid, but you could see clear Leander and his mother weren't doing too poorly in keeping it up. I walked fast around the edge of the yard, behind the grape arbor, under a well-loaded crab-apple tree Leander had climbed once and none too well to show off to me, and into the barn, amongst whose musty hays we had often strayed. Calliostro, Leander's mule and a sweet old boy, gave out a snort when he saw me.

"You want to go on a walk?" I said to him. He snorted again, happy as a lark on its every day off, as I got him out of his stall and gave him a rub with the brush he liked so well then put his harness on. There was a bucket of carrots from the garden picked probably that morning and I gave him one, then another. It's nice to watch a mule at his snack. There's a balm to it. You watch a gentle mule eat what you've handed it and it's like you've let your eyes shut down, like you've stayed awake but sneaked in a nap. Calliostro and I were friends. Leander had liked to "see the world a little" when we had our get-togethers, and we almost never took the Dictator, just Calliostro and the wagon Leander's father had used around the farm and to take vegetables to sell in town. Leander had had Calliostro since he was young and there wasn't much on that property he favored more. Many was the time I had hitched him up while Leander waited in the moon-lit wagon, reins already in his hands.

I would have been out and away that evening in not much more than ten minutes, except that when I had gotten Calliostro about halfway hitched, Leander's mother came tapping her cane around the corner of the barn. I had good strong teeth in those days but I'd been so sure she was somewhere down around the church that when she appeared, they just about all of them fell out of my mouth and onto the dusty barn floor. She didn't seem a bit surprised to see me, though, standing there handling her son's mule and her dead husband's wagon. She gave me a smile, asked me if I was thirsty, and lifted up a glass of something looked nice and cold.

"Ma'am?" I said.

"I got iced blackberry tea here. Would you care for some? Wet your whistle? You look like you could use some refreshment. I just made it fresh. Even in some good shade, it's hot out as burned chili beef today."

I didn't know what to say to any of it and waited for whatever trick it was she had in mind to expose itself. She wasn't tall, but she was about as hard-looking as Leander was soft. She had great big blue eyes lurking like holds full of treasure in a wrinkle ship. Her apron sat as crooked as Leander's hairpiece. I didn't like the look of the wiry muscles in her forearms but she was almost as old to look at as that Erastus Fellows's mother and cane-bound on top of it.

"I can just set it down if you don't want it now," she said. "Drink it up when you get Calliostro ready to roll. He's a good boy, ain't he? He can pull all day. As big a load as you like. My old husband got him for my Homer when he wasn't much more than ten years old."

"Are you Mrs. Hale, Mr. Hale's mother?" I said. I said it like it was a question but of course it wasn't one, even if I had never seen her up close outside of a picture Leander had shown me a few times. The picture was in a locket he kept on him. Even when we were in the hay. I bet he had had it in the ditch. It was an old picture, and she had been wearing her

239

Sunday clothes and a little hat about covered up in grapes, but setting the wrinkles aside, she hadn't changed much.

"Yes, he is my foolish and lazy son, the only one I got. He sent you over here, didn't he? Lazy like a lord as he is."

"Ma'am?" I said.

"He sends all kinds over to bring back his conveyance. What did he give you, a nickel?" She got a kind of squinty look in her eye when she said this. Like she was counting the change in his and her pockets both.

"He gave me a quarter," I said.

"He never did! A whole quarter!" she said.

"Well, anyway, he said he would give me a quarter when I came back with his mule and cart."

She smiled and nodded. This arrangement seemed to suit her better.

"Do you want this drink or don't you? I expect he had you cut through the fields to get here. I saw you come up from the pond. He likes that pond and knows all the shortcuts, that boy. He wants to rise up on out of here, but he'll never forget this place, that's sure. Place like this glues itself to your bones; you don't scrape it off. He is sharp as a tack but too lazy by a long mile. He needs to work on that. Don't you think he's lazy?"

"He had a hundred people listen to his speech."

"Did you listen to his speech?"

"Not much. Some."

"I hear he gives a good speech. I don't listen to any of them, though. I make him practice out here in the barn. This mule has heard it all. My heart don't tick right and I can't afford to get riled up. He riles them up, don't he?"

"They were all cheering."

She nodded. "You've got a scratch on your forehead. You want something for that?"

I shook my head. She made a remark about the paint smears and splatter I had on me, said she expected they had come from the festivities, and I went over to her and took the glass. It was sweating in the heat but as cool inside as the bottom of the pond. I drank down what was in there in one good, long gulp. When I was done I went to set the glass down beside the door, but she gave me a glare and said to hand it back to her. It wasn't every cornsilk woman in the world would take a glass a cornflower or any other had sipped from and I looked at her a little carefully before I put it in her hand.

"You think it strange, do you?" she said.

"A little."

"I don't blame you. Who wouldn't?"

I nodded. We stood there looking at the glass in her hands. It looked like a piece of a life you could live in. Place cool and small and sweet-smelling that had opened itself up.

"You better get on," she said.

"All right."

"There's a pump you can clean yourself up at."

"I don't mind."

"Anyways, take that water jug with you, it's hot out." She pointed at a jug sitting next to a rusted hoe and a feed cart. "I got Homer to fill that up this morning. Might even still be cool. He didn't want to take the wagon into town so he left it sit here. Didn't think anyone ought to see he didn't have anything but a wagon to ride in."

She chuckled. "Guess he has changed his mind. You bring it with you, now."

"He's taking folks to Marvel, Mr. Hale is," I said as I hefted up the jug and set it in the back of the wagon.

"I know it," she said. "I know about the buses too. Since I paid for them out of money we don't have. I would go if I could. Don't make any mistake about that. Don't mean I don't offer blackberry tea to strangers doing paid favors for my only son."

We both looked at each other. She pursed her lips. "Especially if they aren't strangers. Especially if I've seen them before."

"All right," I said. I said it slowly, trying to puzzle from the look on her face whether this was the trap after all and it had just been slow in closing its jaws.

But she just said "All right" too, then said that at least her big lazy boy had good taste in the look of his ladies even if they were too young and good taste was about all he had.

"You tell him to knock on my door when he gets home, doesn't matter how late it is. I won't be asleep," she said.

"He doesn't know I'm taking his wagon," I said.

"It's his mule but it's not his wagon and never you mind. These things work themselves out. All of it works itself out. I've been around the field a few times. My man's sleeping in his bone suit and I haven't been young in many a long year but I remember. There's nights plenty I lay myself down and my heart starts to hammering like I was a girl again. Like he wasn't gone. Like we still had the whole row to hoe."

She had let her eyes go drifty when she said this but they didn't stay drifty for long.

"That goddamned row," she said. "Wear gloves if you've got them. Working it'll blister you up."

She laughed and I laughed some with her.

Then I stopped laughing and said, "I had a thing I wanted to tell him."

"And did you?"

"I think so."

"Well, then, that's a start."

"Yes, ma'am."

"You don't need to *ma'am* me. My name is Leona."

"Mrs. Hale."

"That works just fine too."

"My name is Calla. Calla Destry."

"I've been pleased to meet you, Miss Destry."

"Do you want to keep the water jug here, Mrs. Hale?"

"No, I do not. There is nothing special about it and I reckon you'll be just as thirsty wherever it is you're going as he will."

I cried some more then. I didn't like to do it there in front of her, but she didn't seem to mind and just nodded and looked me in the eye when I said I didn't know what it was I was crying about.

"I don't cry," I said when I had myself back under control.

"I expect that's true," she said.

"It must be the heat."

"You think it's the heat?"

"No. Not the heat."

I might of kept talking and who knows what I would have come up with—mop doll, wrecked buses, the gun in my basket—but she held up her hand to stop me, and I expect we were both grateful that I did.

"You be nice to that mule," she said. "He's a sweet old thing."

"I know it," I said.

"If you don't want to ride out through town, you better take the back lane. But you probably already had that figured."

I nodded. With her cane hooked over her wiry forearm, she helped me finish getting Calliostro hitched, pulled the barn doors wide, then stood watching as I climbed up and took the reins in hand.

I had to jump down off the wagon twice to open and close gates as I left the Hale property. Some ache had set in and each time I climbed back up my wrist hollered and my head called out for help. The lane along the back of their land was grassy and smooth, but the road it gave out onto wasn't, and the sun, low as it was getting, was still beating hard and heavy. I kept a good watch on the surrounds but didn't see a soul the whole time I rode. There were turkey vultures wheeling on whatever sick gusts and breezes might be haunting the heights, and I saw some deer standing still in an empty cow pasture. Pigs there were aplenty, all of them on their sides in the mud like they had been knocked down and hadn't yet been given leave to get back up.

A cloud of gnats came along for some of the ride. They gave out their screams and tried their luck at worrying at my scrapes. I had a thick streak of green paint up near my elbow and one of them landed in its middle and got stuck. Calliostro had some flies and gnats of his own at his ears but he seemed happier than ever to be out in the air and cruising the countryside. Floating brisk across the quiet fields. The wagon was big but built light, and its wheels rolled smooth and true.

I tried to work out if I was happy or mad or something else in between that my try at stealing from Leander had ended up the way it had. And how had it even ended up? There I rode out of Ryansville with the leave of the property's mistress; that's about all that was clear. The jug of water sloshed heavy behind me. Made me wonder after a floaty while whether they got enough to drink in the big beyond.

Christ the carpenter had been thirsty and they had given him vinegar to drink. Held it up to his mouth with a long stick. What was it about cornsilks gave them the idea they needed to lift people up into the air to kill them? Their saints and their sinners both. Cornflowers did their killing on the ground. The killings I had heard about, anyway. What would those boys feel later when they went to their ends? Probably just fear. Fear and evil all around and up with them into the air. Would they still be awake? Or would they rise unconscious? Scared into their long dreaming. I hadn't read the paper yet, hadn't heard any accounts to turn the sky of my memories black and send me drifting forward through the dark. That would be during the days to come. I had ascension and my own troubles and not much more on my mind when I rolled into the evening and down the shabby lane that would lead to Big Bob's fishing spot.

I saw it first, small fires scattered through a wide stand of trees, almost a woods, and then heard it, through crickets and katydids, a murmuring and a crackling and the little sounds of people shifting on stumps and branches and seats of grass and earth. I counted more than a dozen neat fires as Callio-stro took me down the smooth tracks, though some of them may have been doubled up by the surface of the wide, reedy pond. Out of which many a line had pulled fish if the smell everywhere now of sweet, wet roasting was any indication. They had sticks over their fires and whole fish or heavy chunks of fish meat set to scorch, the cornflowers that had gathered under those trees, and there was smoke in the air, smoke and fish steam both.

The lane doubled back on itself and went over a little stone bridge, then widened out and I saw a meadow where I could leave Calliostro. He snorted and flicked his ears when I told him I would be back soon. I took my basket, gave him some carrot to chew, then left him to rest in shadow and stepped into the cool of the woods, dusk come early inside them. I passed small fires as I went, and at each fire tired faces, slick with sweat but breathing slow, food in hand and the storm at least for the minute a way off behind them.

It was Bob's bright little snaggletoothed dog that let me know after I had wandered awhile that Bob was there. She gave out some loud barks and came running over and spun around and jumped up against my leg and wagged her tail like we were old friends. I followed her and found Big Bob grilling chunks of fish on a stick he was holding out over his own neat fire. It was a pretty picture. I can call it up clear, right here, right now, and only its own dark, natural dark, good clean dark of settling dusk. Man with food to eat and a fire to cook it over. Close to the others but not too close. Each at their own flame. Prettier all of it by far than Christ and his cross and scared-to-death boys and all that vinegar.

"Ho there, Calla Destry," Bob said. Said it quiet. Like the only right way you could talk in these woods by this water was to whisper.

"Ho there, Big Bob," I said nice and quiet back.

Bob patted his leg and Myrtle jumped up and curled into his lap.

"How's your finger?" I asked.

"Not much better."

"You sitting over here at your fire thinking about your oranges?"

"Care for another taste?" He held out the hand wasn't holding a stick, held it out empty, and there by some magic of the evening a sliced orange sat.

"You could eat on those all day," I said, putting down my basket and pretending to take a piece and chew.

"I'm telling you," he said.

We sat awhile. I asked him how he had made out with the boys had come looking for me and Bob spit and asked me the same thing back. "All right," I said. He asked me if I had lost them. Or used my fists on them. "Neither one," I said. He said it looked like I'd got in a fight with some paint cans. I told him I had tried to wipe some of it off. He asked if it was really, truly me had rigged that mop to look like a girl. Hung it from the courthouse. Indiana sweetheart. He smiled some when he said that

248

last and there was a little cracked tooth gleaming at the corner of his smile and in that little cracked tooth I reckoned I could read just about all the whole story of both our days. I asked him what he had done to get himself locked up for sixteen hours in a tin shed in Georgia and he said that like me he had stood up when he was supposed to stay sat down. "That's why I like you," he said. I gave him some more of my answers. And funny thing, they all seemed for a while to go swooping in and around Ben Able and Robert True riding along on my running boards. Bob said speaking of which he saw I wasn't riding in the Dictator. I said that that was right, I wasn't, I didn't have it anymore.

I think we were both too tired to talk but we talked and at the same time sat somehow quiet and Bob said it wasn't just imaginary oranges he had to offer and handed me over his stick stuck heavy with fish. I pulled off a hot, slippery piece. I was worried in the low light he might be handing me catfish and I'd have to chew and think the whole time about Leander and the church folk and my plate tossed into the rose of Sharon, but it was bass or some fat bluegill and goddamn if it didn't taste almost too good. We ate, Bob setting down the stick and slipping half his share to Myrtle, who whined and fussed while she chewed. When we were finished and had sat still awhile and gathered some more dusk and quiet up around us, Bob squinted his eyes and said, "I wasn't thinking about oranges till you came over here."

"I didn't think you were. I hope I didn't break your train of thought."

"Leastways not beyond repair."

"Nothing like a broken thought."

"When you don't have the right tools."

"Don't you wish sometimes all it took was a wrench?"

"I like that notion."

"It's a good one, sure."

"But my thought isn't broken. I'm still thinking it. Even as we're talking, even as we're sitting here. It's about cemeteries," Bob said.

I tilted my head. Bob said he expected it sounded strange. I said it wasn't the strangest thing I'd heard that day.

"You reckon they've done it yet? The deed? Lifted up those boys?" I asked.

Bob shrugged.

"I wanted to bust them out."

"'Course you did."

"It's true." I said this and felt it, suddenly, through every speck of myself. Feeling it made me shiver and want to stand up and break something and not scream this time but howl. But there we all were, sitting in the stand of trees, so what I did was nod and make a fist and then let it go.

"I wonder where they'll let them rest," Bob said. "Once they're done with them."

"Our place, I expect."

"Did you know we've got more than one?"

"What?" I was still thinking about howling and breaking things besides bus outings but I was listening too.

"Here's what I was thinking on," he said.

Bob leaned over and picked up his cooking stick. He brushed the ground to the side of the fire clear, then started poking and scraping at it. He made ten marks, then leaned back. Then he leaned forward again, scratched it all out, and set the stick down again.

"You know that mess of a map I was working on?"

"Didn't look like a mess to me."

He reached behind him, groped a minute, leaned way back, and, without dislodging Myrtle, fetched back up with the thing in his hand. "First I thought I would leave it back home. Safe, I hoped. But then I thought maybe those boys come back and maybe they burn the place down. You can't know. You walk out your door and you can't be sure. That's just the way of the motherfucker. And I didn't want to lose my thinking on this." He pulled off the rubber band had been holding it tight and unrolled the map. Told me to come around to his side of the fire so I could see better. Bob smelled like sweet corn, sweet barley; like good-cooked fish and smoke. If Myrtle minded having that map lying on top of her and me leaning over Bob's shoulder, she didn't show it.

Bob had kept working since I'd been to his bait shop, and the map had grown its frame of faces. There must have been fifty cornflowers and cornroots too around that map's edges. Looking up out at us. Bob had pasted a old, blurry picture of the courthouse in its middle. He said it had taken him a while to decide to do it but when he had, it had seemed just right.

251

"You see all those black marks?" he asked. "Spread all out and scattered over the countryside?"

As he pointed I could see his pinkie finger. It was still swollen plenty. I touched at a couple of the black marks. I had green and yellow spots on the back of my hand. I nodded.

"Those are graveyards," he said. "They're ours or they're old cornroot burying grounds. Spread out across the county. Around home."

"Cornroot burying grounds?"

"'Course. Who do you think all this country belonged to. Big one's out near where they fought the Battle of Mississinewa. We widen out the scale, see, and find plenty more. More of ours too. These are the ones in the vicinity. According to my researches."

"So this is a map of the county."

"It's bigger than the county."

"You have been thinking about this."

"I'm always thinking, aren't you?"

"I'm always trying not to."

"This is just the map part. I've got a scale model in the back room at home."

"Of graveyards?"

"That's what I'm telling you."

It wasn't just pictures the map had grown since I'd seen it earlier. There were silver lines across it and colored flourishes too.

"You need to listen up now, Calla Destry."

252

"All right."

"You need to watch," he said. "We're just out here at the fishing hole and losing light and that fire's flickering awful and we can't see too well, but watch anyway."

I leaned forward. Bob began tracing the silver lines he'd made between the black marks. He squished down on Myrtle some as he did his tracing but she stayed still. By and by he had traced the lines between all the marks, and then he put his index finger down on the picture at the middle.

"That's why it seemed right to paste on the picture of the courthouse," he said.

"It's where all the lines cross," I said.

"Makes a star right there at Marvel. Right at the middle. It's the crux."

"The crux?"

"Middle of the ghost roads."

"I don't know what that means."

"I don't either but it's the ghost highways. It's where they walk. It all goes through Marvel."

"What are the pictures for? Of the cornflowers?"

"To show that we know. That we see. That we're here."

"Show who?"

"Whoever looks at it."

"But what if you drew the lines a different way?"

"This is the way it's done. The way I've done it. Make a star from your specks and find the star's heart. I'm just trying to figure it."

"In your figuring is there anything we can do?"

"It's just how it is."

"The way of the world."

"The way of the world, that's right."

I had my mouth ready to make another question but at that minute Myrtle lifted her head and gave out a sharp bark.

"You see!" said Bob. "Even old Myrtle agrees."

"Agrees with *what?*" It was a little old man. Walking over to us with a apple in his hand. He put the apple to his mouth and bit down with a bright crunch and said he and his were looking for a ride over to the prayer vigil. Bob smiled and shook his head and the old man walked off to the next fire.

"Prayer vigil?" I said.

"Against the lynching. That's what they're saying, anyway. At an old Quaker meetinghouse not too far off."

"I met a Quaker earlier. Said he was a Quaker."

"Was that before or after you punched a bus and went swimming in some paint?"

"I didn't punch a bus."

"Might as well have."

"I'd have broke my hand."

"Instead you broke a car."

He laughed then. Long and loud. I could see heads turning our way.

"Aren't they all already doing that, praying, right here, praying at their fires?" I asked when he had got quiet again.

Bob looked around and then back at me but didn't answer.

"Are you going?" I said.

Bob shook his head. He shook it more than he needed to, like he had got started back in thinking about his ghost roads and had forgot to stop. He was still shaking his head—but just tiny movements, you could barely see them, and maybe his eyes were closed, closed and thinking about ghosts and oranges—when I got it into my mind that maybe I'd find Aunt V and Uncle D at that prayer vigil, that if they hadn't come here, that was where they must have gone. Meaning that was where I had to go too. Tell Uncle D I had wrecked his Dictator. Tell him I was sorry I had taken his gun. Tell Aunt V that she was right. That I *was* in trouble. That I *had* gone looking for the devil. That it wasn't ending well. It hadn't helped at all telling Leander what I had needed to tell him. Surely talking to Uncle D and Aunt V would be different. I would tell them everything and I would apologize for everything and they would listen and then we would find our way home together. After we had bowed our heads. I didn't mind bowing my head. Hortensia and I had gone to church together every Sunday when we were still at the orphan house. Bowing your head was better by far than getting beat to sleep and yanked up into the air.

I told Bob I thought I might just find my missing family at the Quaker house, and he opened up his eyes, or at least looked at me again, and smiled and said that maybe, yes, they had gone there, that maybe that was so. It was a big night and full of mysteries, he said, and maybe that was just exactly where they had traveled along their own stretch of the evening road. There wasn't any way to be sure until I had gone and looked but he could see I had to try.

Bob's words and the idea that I might find Aunt V and Uncle D at the vigil and tell them everything and that I was sorry — for stealing money, for taking the car, for taking the gun, for telling them that morning to go to hell, for getting myself into exactly the kind of trouble they had tried to keep me out of — and ask them to take me back and not give up on me no matter what I did and no matter how much I cursed them, and maybe the fact on top of it that I finally had some food in my stomach, made me so happy I hugged Bob right over the top of Myrtle and got growled and bit at by her. Bob hugged me back a little, then I kissed him on his cheek and picked up my basket and told him I was going to fix everything.

"Everything, is it?" he said.

"Everything."

"Everything is an awful lot."

"I know it."

I laughed. He didn't.

"Take this," he said. He tapped the map with his finger, then rolled it up and put the rubber band back on it.

"I can't take that."

"Borrow it for a while. Might not lead you right but it can show you clear where you shouldn't go. Not tonight. Not while it's dark."

"I couldn't."

"You decide to go on somewhere from the church, you can leave it there. Leave it with Desmond if that's where they are. I'd like his opinion on it anyway."

"What do you think he'll say?"

"What he always does."

He winked but didn't say what that was and I let him put the map in my hand, hand with the paint splotches on it, told him I'd take good care of it, hugged him again, and went walking off fast through the fires. On the way I passed that old man with the apple and told him I had a wagon and was heading to the vigil if he wanted to come. He did, Lord, yes, he said, and five minutes later it was me with fixing everything on my mind and that old man and his three women kin riding up the lane for the prayer vigil behind Calliostro.

It had been nice in the trees by the water with the fires and smells and sounds of cooking fish but it was nice too out on the evening road, listening now to the crickets and to Calliostro's hooves on the gravel, now to the creak of the wheels and a swirl of sleepy wrens replaying their day in a stand of nearby hickories. The old man's name was Jasper, he said, and the older woman with him was Miss Marjorie Keys. The two of them sat up on the front bench with me. The other two sat behind and didn't give their names but after a while one of them asked into the noisy country quiet if we thought praying could help those boys. Jasper said if anything could help those boys over in the jail, if they were even still in the jail, it was mighty prayer, and when he said this, Miss Marjorie gave out a deep sigh and began to sing. She sang and after a while the two others on the bench behind began to sing too. And it was nice and it was pleasant. Nice and pleasant to ride along in that wagon with those women singing. Ride with the sound of the crickets and song and to be just sitting there behind Calliostro with Big Bob's map and my basket at my feet.

The song came to a close and Miss Marjorie went quiet but

the two behind us took up again so soft you could hardly hear them and after a while of rolling like this Miss Marjorie said, "There is the world and then there is what is in it and that's not the same thing." Jasper nodded and patted her on the leg like he had heard it before and then she said, "I once had a cornsilk woman I had never seen before tell me what the ground ought to do was just open itself up and swallow me and every other kind of corn wasn't silk that there was. Ought to recognize its mistake and take us back unto itself. They say things like that. Stand around next to them and they say it. Just comes out. Maybe not every last one of them, but enough. Enough to make it true. Is it true? Am I lying now?"

"No, ma'am," said the two women behind us. They said it then went back to their singing.

"Still, I'm done being sad tonight and I plan to be done forever. How does that sound? Does that sound good to you all? How 'bout to you, young Miss Calla Destry?"

"Can't be done forever, Marjorie. It doesn't work that way," said Jasper.

"Then how about for a little while? How about for right now? On our way to this vigil."

"For just right now?" asked Jasper.

"Just for this minute. Till we get there. Does that sound good to you girls?"

I nodded. The two behind me did too. They hadn't stopped singing. And before we had gone another ten feet Miss Marjorie had joined in their singing and we were just rolling along through the night, not sad or anyway saying we weren't. I would have liked to roll along like that forever, and thought a few good times as we went rattling that maybe we'd slipped over into something a little better than it had just been and than it was about to be, that we had slipped all five of us into some small hurt heaven wasn't anybody's but our own.

Good feeling or not, ten minutes later it came upon me that I needed the bushes just about as badly as I had ever needed anything in my life, and I handed the reins to Jasper and was off the wagon with my basket and heading for cover before anyone had time to much more than notice I was going.

"Where's the fire, girl?" said Miss Marjorie.

"I'll catch up, you just keep on!" I said.

"There's a tight turn up here a little ways, we'll meet you on the other side," said Jasper.

"Calliostro can make any turn if you lead him right!" I called.

"Look at her go!" said Miss Marjorie.

Leander called that kind of bush work "making your opinion known." "Excuse me, I have to share my opinion, my beloved," he liked to say. He had a delicate stomach and it came upon him plenty often. *Had* come upon him plenty often; bent over there myself and feeling sorry to see Bob's fish go, I forgot a minute I was done with all that. I forgot other things too. Like those boys in that jail. They lived once. They were real. Fool boys, that's all. Got into trouble. What do you expect? Maybe even done some of what they said. But air killings?

It was cornflowers and cornsilks both supposed to be at the prayer vigil we were heading to. Jasper had said that as we climbed into the wagon. I got worried as I sat down a minute to wipe my eyes and stop my head spinning—even nice and pleasant as I had been feeling—that I might walk in the door and put my fist in the face or worse of the first cornsilk I saw. Then I wished I still had mop doll so I could knock every cornsilk at that prayer vigil upside the head with her. Every cornflower too. I shouldn't have left the fires. I'd left happy and dreaming about reunions and feeling good and now here I was. Must have been the wagon bouncing had sent me this way. Fuck Leander. Fuck confessions. Fuck asking Aunt V and Uncle D to take me back. Fuck Leona Hale and her wrinkles and her blackberry tea. I'd go find Roscoe. Raise my child up right. I raised my child up right. All I needed from Leander was money. That's what the gun had been for. Could still be for. I straightened up and felt its weight in the basket. So I pulled it out.

Pointed its blue barrel at my face. Held it there a good long time. "Don't you dare take that gun of mine, Calla Destry," Uncle D had called after me that morning as I left the house. "You take it and we won't be here when you get back." I let it rest against my forehead, the gun I had taken anyway, for I needed something, anything, that would look close at me and tell me what it saw.

261

THE ANGEL
RUNNER

So I said my good-byes to them and they went off on their way and I hoped to myself it was a fair way, though I did not like where they were going and thought they would probably go to hell for it. I allowed myself one little look at Bud Lancer over my shoulder—because unless you're Lot's wife, one little look is always allowed—but Bud was dancing around in a circle with Ottie Lee and I could not see them either one very well.

It wasn't much of a walk back over to the church, where I found them all still sitting there so peaceful and more coming in every minute. Earlier we'd had Homer Hale in to set with us awhile although he hadn't lasted any much longer than it had taken for some of us to convince the crowd that had chased him straight up to the church doors to go away. He had been considerable excited at the start and had flopped around like a big hooked fish and said loud he had made mistakes and many of them but that he was a good Christian underneath and had drawn pursuers away from his beloved and would we give him haven in his disgrace. We said we would, sure, but that it wasn't a talking vigil and he needed just to sit quiet a spell. We were praying for the poor boys up in Marvel and for the poor world they and many among our

265

number had to do their living in, we told him. If he had played some part, as we just about all had, in the poor quality of it, he could stop his fish-flopping and think on that. After we said that he sat quiet sure enough for a little while and mostly stopped his flopping and prayed, or anyways bent over his head and breathed heavy and dripped some good sweat with us on his lap.

Homer Hale was gone now, though, and Bud and Ottie Lee and Pops and Dale were gone too, and I saw Veronia and Desmond Combs from Marvel had come in and were sitting soft and quiet and leaned up against each other like any other way they would fall. I went in past a pair of quiet-talking women I hadn't met yet discussing a Klan gathering being planned just south of Marvel town and how they were streaming in now from everywhere and we would have to pray even harder to keep that evil down. They were holding hands as they talked. I took a seat for a while near the back of the house where someone had set a pot of dusky-pink carnations.

I sat with my head bowed and I prayed for those boys in the jailhouse just like my angels had taught me, which was by counting to ten and not skipping any decimals. They had told me that each time I prayed, I must pick up where I had left off. I had got about to the middle point between 1 and 1.5. It was a good way to pray because I knew I would get it wrong from the start because you just can't count all the numbers and getting it wrong is a kind of love because getting it wrong teaches you and teaching you is a kind of love and love is always good—my dead father told me that—it is what Jesus taught.

I did my praying and then I lifted up my head because counting had put it in my mind that we needed to increase the flock. I looked around at the heads bowed and the hands good and clasped and put my own head back down and clasped up my own hands again because maybe what I really meant to myself by increasing the flock was that I wanted to see Bud Lancer again, for I am weak just like we all are. That I wanted to go back out into the night and track Ottie Lee and Bud and Pops and Dale down. Who hadn't been anything like nice when they had been here. Who had done nothing but snicker and were probably, friends of mine though I counted them, like I counted all people, or just about all, on their way to hell. But I was good at tracking. I liked to track. I thought I could find anything and anyone.

My truck was back from being borrowed so I started it up and went driving nice and tidy down the road. I'd had my motivating thought—which was nothing direct to do with Bud Lancer or Ottie Lee Henshaw—and it was that I needed to see if old Esther Cotton wanted to come to the vigil. Old Esther Cotton hadn't slept to speak of in years and would be wide awake and talking to the moon. I sometimes took her out for a run in the truck with me and she never said too much of anything or smiled much but she was still right smart and fine company.

I always took her out on the smooth roads because she was

about the oldest piece of a carapace I knew and bumps in the road were not kind on her. I had not thought of her before in the church and I felt bad for that, but now I had. I drove down the road and did not look for Bud or Ottie Lee. I just about knew where they were, because I knew where they had been heading and all the good roads to get there, and to get anywhere, then and now, but I did not drive that way.

I drove instead toward the moon, then away from it, then toward it again. Esther Cotton liked to tell her stories to the moon. She had lived out a few stories in her day and said when she did say anything that there wasn't anything better than telling them to the bodies of heaven, that they always listened and never answered and you couldn't cook it up much better than that. I said she could tell me any stories she liked while we were riding and I wouldn't answer but she looked over at me and shook her head. She said she would not tell me her stories about what she had done and who she had been if that is what I was asking but that she would tell me where she was from, which was way over in Randolph County, and that she had once had a husband and had had her adventures and had long been involved in stock husbandry and basic crop farming and in all the ways of tending the earth.

I drove through the night toward Esther Cotton's little corner, which she had bought from Vic Dunn not ten years before. If she was up she would come with me or would anyway appreciate being asked. I did not like any part of the way Bud Lancer acted or who he was in the world or anything except that he had put his hand tender and soft on my face once. He had done it and called me fine and good in the shed out behind my father's workshop. He had been young and I had been young and he had put his hand on my face and I had put my hand on his hand and shut my eyes. Not long after, I had my accident and got hit on the head and started seeing my sweet angels and had one eye knocked crooked and you couldn't blame him if he found someone else and never put his hand soft upon my face again.

Esther Cotton's light was out and her door was dead to my knock and Colonel, her beat-down bluetick, was tied up tight under the spirea bush. Colonel and I were friends and he gave my hand a lick when I offered it over to him. There wasn't anything young about him either. He gave my hand another slow lick then put his head back down and wagged his tail stump and shut his droopy lids. I said, "Good soldier," like Esther Cotton always said, quiet, so as not to excite him, and knocked again, hard with my fist, because Esther Cotton had told me I should whenever I came calling, but she didn't answer. "She hasn't gone and died on us, has she, Colonel?" I said. I said it with a laugh because I didn't want to believe it and loud enough for him to hear me but not so loud he didn't have to answer if he didn't want to. He didn't want to. So I decided probably she was just asleep, despite what she liked to say about never sleeping, or else she was talking her stories to the moon too loud to hear me, so I got in my truck and drove off again.

I thought I knew about where Bud—who was alone in the world now and so what could it hurt—and Ottie Lee would be by that time but I didn't go that way. I went north and east and I went fast like I practically always do. There were folks of all shapes and stripes out and about, walking in the dark on the roads between the fields, and some in cars, but none I knew to name. I was eye-flipping and neck-stretching so much I about didn't see the boy sitting by the side of the lane. Point of fact, I was past him near a hundred yards when I realized he hadn't been a bush or a stump but a someone and possibly in need of my help. I always help people if I can. It's just what I do. I stopped and shut off the truck. It popped and hissed a time or two, then I got out and walked back toward him.

I didn't walk too fast because you don't do that when you don't know who it is you are walking toward and they don't know you. Also I am aware that because I am tall and have big shoulders and that eye of mine that woggles and scared off Bud, I can scare other people too. Esther Cotton had said more than once to me that she liked it that I was tall and could scare people with my eye and shoulders and that she would like to watch me do it sometime and that she had once herself been capable of creating a similar effect, but I told her that much as I loved her, it wasn't right to scare people, plain and simple. So I walked slowly and stooped in my shoulders a little as I came up on that boy.

He was a bigger-looking person when I got up on him than

he had looked as I went walking up his way through the dark, just plain big, even, but he was still nothing but a young-faced cornflower boy, seventeen or eighteen at best. He was sitting cross-legged with his hands in his lap. There was a bicycle, of all things, lying on the ground next to him. He had a whistle on a string around his neck.

"You catch a sharp rock in your tire?" I asked him. I smiled when I said it. I know I smiled because I always do.

"I say, is your bicycle ailing or are you just taking the air? It's warm enough to, I know it. It ain't hot like it was and at least you can breathe." I had kind of crab-crouched down next to him and now I let myself all the way down onto the ground. Up the road, my truck gave out another pop. I looked up but the boy didn't.

"What's your name?" I asked him this because my angels had told me that I must know my neighbor, and I liked to do my best.

"Roscoe," said the boy. He said it looking straight out over the road and on over the fields the way you look when you aren't looking at anything but the specks set to floating in your own eyes.

"Is your bicycle hurt? Did you fall off it?"

"I could ride a thousand miles on that contraption and not fall off it. I rode it all the way up from Indianapolis."

"Well, now," I said.

"But I won't ride it, not no more. I won't ride it another inch."

"We could put it in the back of my truck. I could fetch it over there and put it in if you're tired. I'll drop you where you need to get. Or you could come back with me to the prayer vigil. Do you like to pray?"

"Who are you?" He said this a little like it had just come upon him that I was sitting there. Old Esther did this sometimes. I knew other folks did it too.

"Why, I'm Sally Gunner from over near Frankfort. My mother was Mary Ellen Gunner and they always called my father Handsome Tom. I don't know you but I know plenty of folks down in Indianapolis. Where do you live? Were you visiting in Indianapolis or coming back from there? Who are your folks? I'd be proud to help you. I've been just about everywhere there is to be around here."

"Have you been to Marvel?"

"Is that where you're from?"

"It's where I went."

"To see the terrible thing?"

"To see someone."

"Did you see him?"

"Her."

"Oh," I said. I said "Oh" because his eyes had gotten harder and softer both when he said *her,* and I know what that particular calibrating of the optic inclinations generally means, at least when it is happening to me.

"No, I didn't," he said. "She was gone. Her people were

gone. The whole street was empty. I would have taken her away from there."

"They left because of it."

"'Course they did."

"Then did you see it?"

He was quiet for a good long while after I asked this question and I started to wonder if he had heard me. He had a fine profile and broad shoulders and great big knuckles on his hands. When he finally spoke up, it sounded like about all the air had been squeezed out of his bellows.

"I saw it," he said, then dipped his shoulders and shook his head. Put his forehead in one of his big-knuckled hands. That was the gesture my daddy had often made in the days after he got told by the doctor that the cancer had come for him. That the cancer was in his stomach and that it had spread and he was going home with it to the Lord. It was a long and angry trip but he got there. My angels would sit with him sometimes. He thought my angels were gnats to wave his free hand through. Or fleas to worry at his scratches and teary eyes.

"About three mile up this road are two dead dogs," said the boy. He had a long arm and he detached his hand from his forehead and pointed with it past me and up the dusty gravel.

"I'm sorry to hear about that too," I said.

"They look like nice dogs. They were just lying in the middle of the road. I couldn't leave them lie there, so I moved them to the side."

"Had they been hit?"

"They were strangled."

"These are calamitous-sounding things you are saying."

"They had on neckties. I don't mean like the kind they got going up in Marvel that they looped up for those fellows. After they had beat them. Did you know they beat them first? They did. One of them they hung out the jail window. The crowd was full of women. I saw one woman that had a baby in her arms give a boy a kick to his head."

"Oh my," I said.

"It was supposed to be three of them. But they just did two. They let the last one live. I heard someone say an angel had spared him."

"An angel!" I said.

The boy turned his head sharp, leaned close, put one of his hands on the meat of my arm, squeezed it harder than I liked, and looked in my eyes.

"You haven't been there," he said.

"To Marvel? Lord, no, not tonight I haven't. You couldn't pay me enough to go there."

"You can see it in their eyes if they have. I could see it in all their eyes."

"So it has happened. They have done it."

"Oh, they've done it," he said. "And if I hadn't kept moving, they might have done me too. There was plenty called out for it as I went past."

He said it, then dropped his hand away from my arm and

pulled his whistle off his chest and put it in his mouth. I didn't have time to put my hands over my ears before he blew it. He blew it again and I had my hands on my ears and when he stopped and let it fall from his lips I touched my hand gently to his shoulder, then took it away again.

"You going to be all right?" I said. "You're not very old. You're not much older, I expect, than they were," I said.

"I stole this bicycle," he said. "And I stole this fucking whistle. I was going to give it to her. Make a gift out of it. I couldn't find her. She wasn't there."

"Well," I said.

"Everyone has ropes in his eyes," he said.

"I've got some water in my truck, you want some water?"

"Even those dogs had ropes in their eyes. I checked. They've still got their eyes open. You can see it yourself. They were there."

He said this, then gave out another shudder, then he jumped up.

"You want that bike I stole, it's yours. It's a good bike. I got offered cash money for it earlier on. It'll get you where you want to go."

"I have a truck. Where can I take you?"

"You ever see a dead dog with ropes in its eyes?"

"I never have."

"Well, I've seen two."

As soon as the boy said that, he left off from me at a run.

"It's a good bike. It'll roll all night if you know how to ride

275

it." He called this over his shoulder. Then he blew on his whistle again and was gone.

I sat there a piece and listened first to that big boy's foot sounds getting smaller and smaller, then to the frogs and night birds calling through the black and the bats swooping for their supper and, somewhere far off, some dog howling that wasn't dead. Listening to that howl I got myself the idea that I needed to go and take a look at those dogs dead down the road, maybe fetch them somewhere and put them under the ground where the turkey vultures couldn't get them, where they wouldn't be breakfast for the crows. I stood up and started for my truck then remembered the bicycle and thought I would throw it in the back—there would still be room for the dogs—and save it for if I ever saw that boy again.

Only thing was when I had pulled it up, I could feel that it was a handsome-balanced thing. Gave me the idea that if I let it go it would just stand up straight by itself. I admire that kind of a mechanism. Calls harmony to mind. Lets you think the world is wrought truer than it is. I put my hands under the center bar and lifted it up off the ground and it didn't weigh much either. I'd had a bicycle once had weighed up toward sixty pounds. This one couldn't have been more than forty. It was a fine contraption like the boy had said and it had a smooth leather seat and I thought I would ride it up to my truck.

I hadn't been cycle riding in some good while of years but

there it was and there I went. The air zipped faster and fresher around my face when I was on it and I was up at my truck in a second. I leaned there against the sideboards a minute and they felt warm in the night and I thought about its pops and pings and wondered if maybe I ought to go and inspect those dead dogs on the bicycle. Swish up about silent to them and not disturb their sleep. I could come back after and get them with the truck.

So I shoved off from my dead father's vehicle and went off down the dark road. There wasn't any light on that bicycle but your eyes get used to the moonlight when they want to and I could see as well as ever I had. I rolled, and the corn went by me and the beans went by me and the barley and the crossroads and the trees and the houses and the sheds. Before it had been nothing but people, but now it was just the night. I had looked good into the eyes of the boy when he had looked into mine and I had seen those ropes he talked about. I wondered as I rode if I had ropes in my own eyes now from seeing his or if you could get them only if you had stood under the tree yourself. Had looked up at what was hanging from the tree. Looked up at the boys.

I was watching as I rolled for those dead dogs but I didn't see them. I was watching too for Bud Lancer and Ottie Lee and Dale and Pops but I did not see them either. I also watched for Esther Cotton for I reckoned now she had left her house and her own dog and was out there somewhere too, but of her I saw no sign.

One time when I went to visit old Esther she was out in the yard and talking to the moon and didn't quit talking even after I'd come up on her and said "Hi" good and loud. She was telling the moon a story about a man out walking who heard his end was waiting around the corner so he changed his direction and went the other way. "You know better than anyone," said old Esther Cotton to the moon, "just how that one ends."

How about this one?